A Flair for
Drama

Deborah L. Garner

A Sadie Kramer Flair Mystery

Deborah Garner

Cranberry Cove Press

A Flair for Drama
by Deborah Garner

Copyright © 2017 Deborah Garner
ALL RIGHTS RESERVED

First Printing – May 2017
ISBN: 978-0-9969960-2-0

Printed in the U.S.A.

Books by Deborah Garner

Above the Bridge
The Moonglow Café
Three Silver Doves
Hutchins Creek Cache
Cranberry Bluff
A Flair for Chardonnay
A Flair for Drama
Mistletoe at Moonglow
Silver Bells at Moonglow

*For all those who love mystery, drama and chocolate –
or any combination of the above.*

CHAPTER ONE

Sadie Kramer stood in front of the theatre and looked up at the ornate concrete edging along the roofline, wondering what kind of drugs the architect was on when he decided gargoyles would be a nice finishing touch. The Seaside Players Theatre was relatively new, as theatres go, prime for modernity, yet some designer somewhere had decided it should resemble half medieval castle, half Disneyland ride. The building had ominous written all over it.

"What do you make of this, Coco?" Sadie looked down at her tote bag as if she expected it to answer. It often did, with either one yip or two, depending on its occupant's mood. She pulled a treat from the left pocket of her leopard print coat and held it just above the tote bag's rim. *One ... two ... three ...* That was all it took for the Yorkie to pop her head out of the bag. "Look at those bizarre creatures up there." Coco's gaze followed her arm, which, in addition to pointing upward, still held the treat. "And there are others, see? On each side of the front door. I have a good mind to pull out my lipstick and slap a little style on their silly faces." Coco lowered her head, leaving only her eyes and a tuft of sandy brown fur in sight, undoubtedly not wanting to turn to vandalism along with her human.

The will-call window looked as foreboding as the rest of the building, leading Sadie to second-guess her decision to attend the performance. It had seemed like a great idea at the time: a quick escape from the San Francisco fog, a leisurely drive south along the California coast and an evening of musical theatre, not to mention a chance to visit an old friend who was involved with the show. Besides, a visit to Monterey was always welcome. If she managed her time wisely, she could slip into Carmel and do some damage at the quaint shops along Ocean Avenue. Even a window-shopping trip could have benefits. She always seemed to find something unique that she could add to the extensive repertoire of fashionable items at her own boutique, Flair, in San Francisco. Now, facing a young woman at the ticket counter whose expression was no more welcoming than the building itself, Sadie wondered if skipping the production and heading straight to the shops might be a better choice.

The young woman, whose nametag said "Penelope," slid a glass window to the side and looked at Sadie expectantly.

"I was invited to watch tonight's dress rehearsal of *Songs to the Sun*, but I also have a ticket for tomorrow's opening night."

"Name, please?" the woman looked at Sadie expectantly. Her hair was dyed a shade of red that matched both her lipstick and nail polish. Sadie's first impression – perhaps from foundation so thick that it resembled pancake makeup – was that a cast member was manning the ticket booth temporarily while a friendlier clerk was taking a break.

"Kramer, Sadie."

The woman flipped through an alphabetical card file, frowning. "Is that Cramer, with a 'C'? I can't find you here."

Sadie shook her head. "No, it's Kramer with a 'K.'"

Sadie imagined the girl muttering, *why didn't you say so in the first place,* as Penelope pulled an envelope out and slid it across the counter. All she actually said was, "Oh, I see. Just one ticket?"

"Yes, that's correct." Sadie coughed to cover a quiet yip.

"I see," Penelope said again, glancing suspiciously at Sadie's tote bag. "You know you don't need your ticket for the dress rehearsal. You could have just picked it up tomorrow."

"This way I won't have to wait in line with the others. My dearest friend is in the show, you see." Sadie paused, certain this revelation would be impressive. "Well, a close friend." She paused again. "A former classmate from grade school."

"Ah," Penelope said, her tone devoid of any hint of interest.

"Her name is Roxy. She's the one who invited me to the dress rehearsal."

"I see," Penelope repeated.

"Well, she's not exactly *in* the show," Sadie admitted. "She works backstage somewhere, doing something, I'm not sure what."

"That's nice," Penelope said, her voice even flatter than before. She reached for the box office window with one arm, prepared to close it.

"Oh, will there be refreshments in the lobby this evening?" Sadie asked. The idea of spending some time with a glass of wine and appetizers was appealing. Chocolate would be even better.

"There will be wine and hors d'oeuvres at intermission tomorrow," Penelope said. "If you're looking for something now, there's a café about a half block away: Curtain Call."

"A clever name," Sadie said as Penelope slid the window shut. "And...thank you," she added, now facing a sheet of glass.

Tucking her ticket envelope into a side pocket on her tote bag, Sadie turned away from the theatre and walked back out to the street. "What do you think, Coco? Right or left? I suppose we could have asked." The dog barked once. "Yes, I agree, she might have told us, but a little exercise will be good for us."

A short stroll in one direction yielded a dry cleaner, neighborhood market, and a pharmacy, as well as a row of newspaper boxes that had seen better days. Retracing her steps, Sadie passed the theatre and continued on, eventually arriving at a café with two petite tables set into the shade of a blue and white striped awning. It resembled one of many sidewalk cafés she and Morris, her late husband, had visited in France. This particular one might well have been plucked right out of the 6th Arrondissement and relocated along the Pacific Coast. So similar was its Parisian appearance that Sadie glanced across the street, half expecting to see a painter with an easel.

The sandwich-board sign on the sidewalk bore a similar look. Chalky vines and flowers in shades of green and rose surrounded a tantalizing list of daily specials and coffee drinks. Deciding that a bowl of corn chowder and a glass of Cabernet would be the perfect pre-rehearsal fare, Sadie stepped into the café and found a seat at a small table alongside a tall shelf unit of imported crackers. She set her tote bag on the floor next to her, hushed a yip, and looked around. Customers occupied most tables, though a few remained empty. A row of bags along the sales counter indicated the café did a healthy to go business, as well. Sadie watched several customers arrive to pick up orders before the young girl manning the register was able to duck around the counter and approach Sadie's table.

"Sorry to keep you waiting." The girl, slender, of medium height, and in her mid-twenties, pulled a notepad and pen from a bistro-style apron. A bright yellow plastic flower crowned the pen, giving the writing utensil a slightly off-balance look. A plastic nametag read "April." "Are you ready to order?" As she waited for an answer, her head swiveled, first at the sound of the café door opening, and then to glance at a nearby table where two men sat hunched across from each other, deep in conversation. Just as quickly she turned back to Sadie. It was as if she had a kind of automatic radar to keep track of all activity.

"Yes, I believe so," Sadie said. "Your menu out front advertises corn chowder. Do you recommend it?"

"Definitely," April replied, already jotting down the request. "It's a house specialty. Anything to drink with that?"

"A glass of Cabernet would be fabulous." Sadie's statement was followed by an almost inaudible whine. "And a few crackers, if possible," she added quickly.

"Crackers come with the soup." Another soft whine followed.

"I'd love a few before," Sadie said, tapping her tote bag lightly with her foot.

"No problem," April said. "I'll bring some with your wine." She stuffed her notepad and pen in an apron pocket and spun away from the table. A zigzag spurt between tables took her back to the front counter, where several customers had lined up, waiting to pay.

"You needn't be so demanding, Coco," Sadie said, addressing her tote bag as simply as a person would speak to someone in the next chair. Rising voices drowned out the Yorkie's response.

"This was a mistake from the beginning," barked a heavy-set man with reddish cheeks at a man half his size. Sadie hoped for his sake that the mop of hair covering half his forehead was a toupee.

"You're worrying too soon, Palmer. We've been over this a dozen times."

"How is it too soon, Mitchell? Ticket sales are abysmal for opening night. We should be sold out."

"I said from the start we should've done a book musical, Palmer, not an original like *Songs to the Sun*. But you wanted to be the one to get a new show off the ground," Mitchell said. "When you go for glory, you're taking a financial risk. You're the numbers guy. This shouldn't be news to you."

"Of course it's not. As you well know, I've backed plenty of shows." He lifted his beer mug and chugged the remaining half.

"Yet you *did* choose to finance it, so give it a chance. Our marketing strategy is solid. You know my company's reputation for publicity. Mitchell Morgan Media is the best there is. We've got radio spots and all the rest set up for this show."

"Give it a chance?" Palmer's voice rose, and then lowered as he leaned closer to Mitchell. "I planned to give it a chance when Nevada Foster was going to play the lead. I never would have backed this show with Brynn Baker. She isn't right for the part. She doesn't have half the talent Nevada does."

They paused as April stopped by their table. "Another draft, Ernie?" Ernie nodded, and April took the empty mug behind the counter. She returned quickly with a full mug and left the men to continue their discussion.

"Ernie Palmer," Sadie whispered to her tote bag. "Big shot financial guy, Coco. I've read about him in the *Chronicle*."

"Sid cast Brynn," Mitchell said matter-of-factly. "That's his prerogative as the director."

Palmer harrumphed, lifted his beer to his mouth, guzzled half and set it down. "I bet he wouldn't have if he'd known she was going to dump him right after he posted the audition results. Anyway, Sid Martin is an idiot. Nevada was perfect for the part."

April passed between the tables, delivering Sadie's order before hustling back up front.

"You're biased, Palmer," Mitchell said. "You just think she's special because *you* discovered her in Vegas, and she's your little up-and-coming star. If Sid had cast her, it would have made you look good. You would have been the star maker. At least she got the understudy job. You should be proud of that. Plus, if Brynn catches the flu or something, Nevada will have a chance to fill in and prove herself. Maybe she'll get the lead in the next show."

"Maybe." Palmer finished his beer and stood up, tossed some bills on the table, and walked out. Mitchell Morgan did the same, leaving Sadie to contemplate the conversation over chowder and wine.

"What do you think, Coco?" Sadie whispered. She picked up a pepper shaker and sprinkled a generous portion into her soup crock. "Maybe there's more to this production than meets the eye. I just love a little intrigue, don't you?"

Coco responded with a series of tiny sneezes. Sadie took a spoonful of soup and blew across it to make sure it was cool. *Yes,* she thought as she relished the first delicious sip. *There's nothing like a little intrigue to turn a weekend trip into an adventure.*

CHAPTER TWO

As the theatre lights dimmed, Sadie settled back in a cushioned chair and kicked off her shoes. Why be uncomfortable when it wasn't necessary? It wasn't like anyone could see to appreciate her new red polka-dot flats anyway. What a steal those had been, eighty percent off, perched high on one of those multi-tiered racks department stores used for shoe sales. She'd also scored a pair of alligator pumps dyed a fabulous bright purple. Those would be perfect for opening night, an ideal match for the purple mohair sweater and black silk pants she planned to wear.

A jeans-clad man wearing a headset walked out to the middle of the stage and welcomed the audience, clearly a stand-in for the person who would fill that role the following night. Sadie looked around, confirming what she'd observed coming in. Other than half a dozen rows in front and a smattering of people throughout the theatre, including in the back, the audience was light.

Two hours and several technical malfunctions later, Sadie stood up and stretched, glad to see the lights come up. The rehearsal had been neither terrible nor great. Only one mishap on stage — a spilled jug of lemonade during a picnic scene in the first act — had caused a brief delay. The show itself, both written and directed by Sidney Martin, was entertaining enough, set around a summer vacation, with various plot threads running between fictional family members. The actors themselves were all fine, including Brynn Baker. Sadie now suspected the director had cast her more for her knockout figure than her talent. Nevada Foster, however, was outstanding in her supporting role. Ernie Palmer, pompous and biased though he seemed, was right about the casting. Nevada would have been a better choice for the lead.

"Psst..." Sadie searched for the source of the hushed sound to find her friend Roxy leaning out of the stage door. "Great to see you! How did you like the show?"

"Very entertaining," Sadie said. "Especially when the lemonade spilled during the picnic scene."

Roxy sighed. "I don't know how that happened, but that scene is too serious, anyway. Maybe we should add that in, though Sid would have my neck if it happened again. Anyway, come on back. Let me show you around."

Gathering her jacket and tote bag, Sadie shuffled sideways until she reached the end of the row, and then met Roxy at the stage door. She blinked as her eyes adjusted to dim lighting inside a narrow stairwell, and then grasped a wooden banister and followed Roxy up the stairs to the stage level.

Sadie had known Roxy for almost sixty years, and although they didn't see each other often, their friendship was like a well-greased pulley, and it was as if they spoke weekly.

"My!" Sadie exclaimed. "It's a whole different world back here. All these ropes and boxes and switches! I never thought about it before. Everything is so neat and organized from the audience's view."

"Exactly," Roxy said. "And it's my job as stage manager to keep it that way. When things run smoothly, the way they should, the audience simply enjoys the show, rather than seeing the chao...well, the inner workings of the production." She paused to greet a good-looking man still in costume and makeup. Sadie recognized him as one of the cast members. "That's Alex Cassidy," Roxy whispered. "Local heartthrob."

"I recognize him from the show," Sadie said. "He has a small part in the first act."

"Yes," Roxy said. "He's Russell Garrett's understudy, so he may get a chance to prove himself."

"The same goes for Nevada Foster, right? She's understudy for Brynn Baker." Sadie looked sideways between two parallel curtains. Two men dressed in black were moving a table across the stage.

"How did you know that?"

"I overheard a conversation at Curtain Call before the rehearsal. Ernie Palmer and another man, someone in charge of marketing."

Roxy snorted. "Those jerks, so arrogant out there in their cushy offices; they have no idea how the theatre really operates. It's all about money and publicity to them. And I'm talking about promoting themselves more than the show, especially Ernie. He and Sid are constantly arguing."

"About Brynn Baker?" Sadie asked.

"About all sorts of things, but Brynn is definitely high on the list." Roxy pulled Sadie aside to allow a stagehand with a cart of electrical cords to pass. "Thanks, Coop," she said before turning back to Sadie. "Dillon Cooper, my right hand guy. Don't know what I'd do without him."

"So Ernie didn't want Brynn to get the lead?" Sadie said. Feeling restless movement in her tote bag, she began to swing it back and forth slightly. "Good shoulder exercise," she said when Roxy stared.

"That's an understatement." Roxy lowered her voice to a whisper and pulled Sadie into an empty dressing room, closing the door. Sadie felt a delicious thrill of anticipation at the prospect of learning about some scandal or other. "Ernie never would have backed the show if he didn't think Nevada Foster would get the lead. Supposedly he had a verbal agreement with Sid to that effect. Sid broke it when he cast Brynn, instead, but the paperwork was already signed and the money guaranteed, and since casting wasn't in writing, Ernie was stuck."

"And then Brynn dumped Sid." Sadie put down her tote bag near the door.

"Wow, you did hear a lot at Curtain Call," Roxy said. "Yes, she dumped Sid for some mystery lover. Everyone thinks it's Russell, but she won't admit it, and he denies it."

"Leading man and leading lady," Sadie mused. "Sort of a cliché, isn't it? Maybe people are jumping to conclusions."

Roxy shrugged. "Maybe. Personally, I think it's Alex, Russell's understudy, though he's way too nice a guy. He deserves better. But I really don't care one way or the other. I try not to get wrapped up in the soap opera around here."

After a sharp knock, the door opened, and Coop stuck his head in. "Sorry to interrupt, Rox, but do you want red or blue lights in that second scene?"

"Blue," Roxy said. "The red is too warm. I don't understand how that got mixed up. It was blue all along."

"The lighting tech said part of the cue sheet was torn off. I'll print and tape down a new one." Coop ducked out, closing the door behind him.

Roxy turned back to Sadie, shaking her head. "It's always something with this show. Listen, where are you staying? Maybe we can get together for a drink later."

"I'm right down the street at a hotel...Seaview... Seaside...Seavista...Seasomething," Sadie said. She bent down and reached into her tote bag, searching for the hotel's registration receipt, knowing the name would be on it, but came up with a Milkbone, instead. She dropped it back in and looked up at Roxy.

"Um. I have a bit of a problem," Sadie said. "I'm missing something from my tote bag. Do you mind if I have a look around the theatre to see if I, um, dropped it on my way back here?"

"No problem," Roxy said. "I really have to finish working, but I know where you're staying. Give me an hour to wrap things up. I'll meet you in the hotel bar. It'll be easier to talk there without the whole crew around at Curtain Call. Can you find your way out?"

"Sure," Sadie said.

Roxy left the dressing room door open, and as she disappeared, she called over her shoulder, "And if you're hungry before then, I recommend the potato skins over that stash of snacks in your purse."

Sadie took a breath, looked in the tote bag again and sighed. No Coco. She left the bag and crept down the hall, peering into dressing rooms, hunting for the little escapee. As she wandered by, some of the actors looked at her curiously, especially since she was hunching over a little so that she could be closer to Coco's level.

Coop came around the corner and stopped in front of her. "Can I help you?"

"No, no, I was just looking around, so curious. Everything back here seems magical." She backed her way down the hall to the dressing room where she and Roxy had been talking, left the door open a crack and stared at her tote bag. There was Coco, gazing at Sadie from the tote, as if she'd been waiting for her for days, looking as if she'd never left.

* * *

The Sea Urchin bore all the trappings of a typical hotel bar: a sleek counter with tall stools, half a dozen circular high tables, a side row of booths, and medium to low lighting. Every few seats a bowl of salty snacks waited, aimed to encourage thirsty guests to linger over refills before retiring to their rooms. A flat-screen television showed recaps of the day's sporting events. Only the fishing nets and model ships on the wall hinted at the watering hole's seaside location.

Sadie sat in an empty booth and ordered the recommended potato skins — "extra cheese, please" — and an Irish coffee — "extra whipped cream, please." She made a mental note of the chocolate lava cake on the menu, which could make a fine after-show treat the next night. It seemed an unusual offering for a bar, but she never judged when it came to chocolate, her biggest addiction.

Slipping a pretzel into her bag, she pulled out her cell phone to check messages. The rhinestones on the hot pink case sparkled under the bar lighting. Given a choice, she would have gone with a zebra print case, or perhaps lime green, but Coco did love pink and, after all, Coco was the one who had to reside with the phone half the time.

There were only three messages on her voicemail, not bad for a full day away from home. Amber, her assistant at her fashion boutique, had called to say the day had been uneventful, though there had been several good sales and Matteo, their favorite chocolatier, had made a new batch of raspberry truffles. The second call was a telemarketer; Sadie hit delete immediately. The last was Roxy, saying she was on the way, a true enough statement, as she slid into the booth just as Sadie put the phone away. Roxy ordered a draft beer, which arrived at the same time as the potato skins.

"Glad the night is over," Roxy said, slumping against the booth's cushion.

The two women had aged differently: Sadie was all soft curves and smiles while Roxy was lean, all sharp elbows and cheekbones, though she had an open, honest face.

"Must be a lot of work, putting on a show like this," Sadie said. She reached for a potato skin and took a bite, closing her eyes and sighing at the thick layer of cheddar cheese. "Gotta love carbs."

"It's not the show itself that's work," Roxy said. "Of course, that *is* work. It's no small feat putting on a full musical like *Songs to the Sun*. But the drama! And I don't mean the show itself. This cast and crew have more theatrics offstage than on. Take Brynn, for example, *such* a prima donna. It's not enough for her to drive Sid crazy, though he drives her crazy, too. She's always demanding special treatment. Even I'm expected to kowtow to her."

"Really?" Sadie finished off one potato skin and started in on another.

"Absolutely," Roxy sighed. "Sid wants her happy, if for no other reason than to keep her from complaining. So when she wants props moved around, we move them. When she wants the lights 'just so,' we adjust them to her wishes. And heaven forbid a curtain rises or falls at the wrong time if it's her entrance or exit."

"Sounds dreadful," Sadie said. "Potato skin?" She held the plate out, setting it back down when Roxy shook her head. "I take it she hasn't made many friends with others in the show."

Roxy laughed. "Hardly, although both Russell and Alex fawn over her like adolescent boys. She loves the attention, of course, so she laps it up. Quite a competition those two have over her."

"Nevada doesn't get the same attention?" Sadie dropped another pretzel in her tote bag, and Coco chirped a thank you.

"Not nearly as much," Roxy said. "She's not as demanding. She's probably the easiest to get along with, pretty easy going. Though…"

"Though what?" Sadie leaned forward, intrigued.

"Well, she has…an edge to her," Roxy said, clearly searching for the right words. "That's the best way I can explain it. It's subtle, but it's there. I figure she resents not getting the lead. Everyone knows she deserved it. Even Brynn, I'm sure. I did overhear her calling Brynn a less than complimentary name tonight when she was talking about her to one of the other actresses. No love is lost between those two, that's for sure."

"That must make things tense," Sadie mused.

"Not for Brynn." Roxy snorted. "She thinks it's funny, and Nevada's mostly subtle anger just feeds Brynn's sense of entitlement. Anyway, it just is what it is." The cell phone she'd placed on the table when she first arrived vibrated. "Sorry," she said, looking at the screen. "It's Coop; I'd better answer." After a short conversation, she disconnected and sighed, turning to Sadie. "The potato skins are all yours. Coop thinks he forgot to lock up the theatre. I need to go back." She stood up, slipped her phone in her pocket and gulped the rest of her beer. "Like I said, it's always something. I'll see you tomorrow. Glad you came down."

"Same here," Sadie said. She watched Roxy leave and dropped one last pretzel into her tote bag. "What do you think, Coco? I'm starting to believe more acting is going on off the stage than on."

Whether the yip that followed was a vote of agreement or a plea for another salty treat, Sadie nodded. "Two, two, two shows in one, Coco. That's what we're getting. The question is: which will turn out to be more interesting?"

CHAPTER THREE

Sadie reached over to the night stand, her hand slapping blindly across the surface, knocking off a pair of rhinestone-studded reading glasses, a dog-eared fashion magazine, and a half consumed bag of peanut butter chocolate cups before landing on her cell phone. Annoyed the *Dragnet* ringtone had interrupted her dream of starring in *Annie*, she looked at the caller ID, surprised to see both that it was 1:30 am and Roxy's phone number on the screen.

Coco stirred in her "palace," an elegant travel crate decked out with silk lining, a velvet pillow and a china water bowl. Sadie soothed her after the quiet whine. She knew Coco hadn't been pleased when she changed the ringtone. But there was only so much "La Bamba" one could take when calls came in. And, after all, Coco had her own favorite music, always Salsa, on her Shuffle, clipped to her collar.

"Roxy?" Sadie sat up and clicked on the bedside light, temporarily startled at the sight of her neon pink flamingo pajamas. Why hadn't she thought to pack the ones with pastel poodles? Those were much less shocking when viewed unexpectedly from a half asleep state.

"What?" Sadie sat up straighter, suddenly wide-awake. Coco lifted her head off the velvet pillow in her crate. "Oh, my!" Sadie stood up. Coco sprang to her paws. "How awful!" She began to pace. Coco mimicked her, changing directions each time Sadie did an about face. The call lasted only a minute, after which Sadie hurried to the restroom to splash cold water on her face while Coco tapped one paw impatiently.

"Coco, we need to go right now," Sadie said as she rushed back into the room. "There's been a terrible accident. Roxy is beside herself. It looks like Nevada will be playing the lead, after all. Oh my, oh my." Sadie shook her head as she traded the pink flamingos for a bright yellow jogging suit. "Oh, my," she said again. She scooped Coco out of the crate and deposited her in the tote bag, tossed in a few treats, and headed to the theatre.

Roxy waited on the sidewalk, uncharacteristically wild eyed and frantic, arms waving. A man who was obviously a plainclothes policeman stood nearby with a notepad and pen. "As I said before," Roxy stated, "I came down to the theatre to check the outside stage door. My assistant thought he might have forgotten to lock it."

"And then what happened, ma'am?" The detective scribbled while waiting for a response. Sadie peeked over his shoulder at the notepad and got an odd look from him. His nametag said, "H. Higgins."

"It's not 'ma'am', officer, it's Roxy, Roxy West. Like Mae West, but without all the curves."

"Yet just as outspoken. And it's 'Detective,' not 'Officer.' Detective Henry Higgins."

"You're kidding," Roxy said.

He ignored her and made another note, stepping away from Sadie as he did. "I'll ask you again: what happened after you came down to the theatre?"

"The door was locked," Roxy said. "So I knew Coop had locked it when he left after all."

"But you decided to go in, anyway."

Roxy crossed her arms. Sadie thought this odd, yet it probably made sense given the detective's accusatory, interrogating tone. The two definitely hadn't gotten off to a good start.

"Yes," Roxy said. "I figured I might as well. I was already here. It made sense to double check everything."

"So you went inside. What happened next?"

"I reached for the light switch, but then realized the lights were already on. That was strange, because Coop would have turned them off before he locked up."

"You're sure about that?" Higgins kept writing.

"Yes, of course I'm sure about it," Roxy huffed.

After Roxy spoke, someone barked twice, and the detective glanced first at Sadie, then at her tote bag, then back to Sadie. She shrugged. He turned back to Roxy. "Go ahead."

Roxy frowned and rubbed her forehead "I'm trying to remember." She raised an arm in the air, as if retracing her attempt to turn on the lights. "When I realized the lights were already on, I called out for Coop, figured maybe he'd decided to come back on his own."

"Even though he'd called to ask you to do it?"

"Yes, why not?" Roxy said. "He's responsible that way. In any case, he didn't answer. No one did. So I went to check the wings, to see if someone else was there and just didn't hear me."

"The wings?" Detective Higgins lifted an eyebrow and kept his pen poised over the notebook.

"The side areas of the stage," Roxy explained. "I thought someone might have left something behind after the rehearsal. And that's when I saw..." She choked up, forcing out the words. "She was just there, in the middle of the stage. I ran over, thinking she'd fainted, but...the blood...it was horrible!"

"Can you verify the victim's name?"

Roxy nodded and stuttered. "Br...Brynn Baker."

"Is there anyone who didn't like Ms. Baker, who had a grievance with her?"

Roxy coughed. "She could be hard to get along with sometimes."

"Thank you. Please don't leave just yet, in case we have other questions." Higgins clicked his pen, inserted it into his suit pocket, and went into the theatre.

"Roxy!" Coop rushed up. His hair was in dire need of a comb, and his jacket hung open, revealing a T-shirt sporting the words "Are you supposed to be touching those props? I didn't think so."

"Thanks for coming down, Coop," Roxy said.

"Of course!" Coop hugged Roxy. "Is it true? Is Brynn ... dead?"

Roxy nodded. She looked both distraught and exhausted, as if the adrenaline rush of the initial shock was wearing off.

"How awful," Coop said. "I couldn't believe it when you called me. Everything seemed fine when I left. I checked all the stage areas carefully."

"You were worried you'd forgotten to lock the door," Sadie pointed out. "Why is that?"

Coop looked from Sadie to Roxy and back to Sadie again.

"I rushed out to meet the rest of the crew at Curtain Call."

"And nothing seemed off to you when you closed up..." Sadie's voice trailed off as she watched the medical examiner's car pull up.

"Who are you?" Coop asked.

"I'm sorry. I saw you backstage tonight, and Roxy told me you're her right-hand man. I'm Sadie Kramer, Roxy's friend."

"Oh, yeah! I know about you. And, no, nothing seemed off. The cast and crew had all left. The theatre was empty. It was like any other night, quiet, at least at that point."

Sadie raised her eyebrows at the last comment. "At least at that point? What about earlier?"

"Well," Coop said, thinking back. "I did hear a lot of shouting from inside Brynn's dressing room just after the rehearsal. But I didn't think much of it. I heard yelling before rehearsal, too. It was probably just Sid reading Brynn the riot act about one thing or another, like always."

"It's true," Roxy said. "That's not unusual. Sid does that all the time, especially since Brynn dumped him. I don't like defending her, but he shouldn't take personal grievances out on people by nitpicking things that have nothing to do with what's really upsetting him."

The conversation paused as Detective Higgins stepped outside the theatre and called out. "Anyone here who can explain some of the stage set-up for our report?"

"I'll go," Coop said, holding up one hand to stop Roxy from responding. "You've had enough trauma for one night." He jogged over to the stage door and disappeared inside with the policeman.

"I should be helping," Roxy said, "But I don't want to go back inside."

"I don't blame you," Sadie said. "It looks like your assistant can handle it."

"Coop? Oh yeah, no question. He knows this theatre inside out, every inch of it. He's worked here for years." Roxy rolled her head from shoulder to shoulder. The move reminded Sadie of something she'd attempted in an exercise class once, back when her doctor had suggested — quite strongly — that she either give up her chocolate addiction or get moving, preferably both. Neither had lasted long, but she did gain several new customers for Flair, classmates who were drawn to her fuchsia workout clothes and light-up sneakers.

Sadie glanced around, spying a low brick wall alongside the next building. "Come sit down, Roxy. I'll stay with you." She led Roxy to the wall and settled beside her. Although eager to help comfort her friend, Sadie's curiosity also fed her desire to linger at the scene. Tragic as it was, this was a sideshow she'd never imagined, a puzzle with multiple possibilities. She wasn't about to miss out. She'd been known on occasion to solve a crime, catching some sort of tiny clue that detectives overlooked.

A black Porsche squealed to an abrupt stop in front of the theatre, and a man Sadie assumed was Sid, the director, jumped out. *How gauche*, Sadie thought. At least her own red Mustang convertible was a classic, not just a fancy car for show. So far she'd heard nothing to endear her to the show's director. The flashy vehicle didn't help the matter.

"I think your director is here," Sadie said. "Wonder how he knew? The police must have called him."

"No," Roxy said. "I called him right after I dialed 911. He doesn't even have twenty-four hours to pull the show back together. He'd have my neck if I didn't get him on it right away."

Sadie looked at Roxy with surprise. "You mean the show will still open tomorrow night? Er, I mean tonight, I guess. Even after this?"

"I'm sure it will." Roxy let out a laugh that sounded half humorous and half resigned. "You know what they say: 'The show must go on.' I'm sure we'll have some sort of emergency meeting in the morning, but that will be the decision. If only because of Sid's ego and Ernie Palmer's refusal to risk losing money."

Coop emerged from the theatre just as Sid approached, almost knocking a paper cup out of Sid's hand.

"It looks like your director stopped for coffee on the way down here," Sadie observed. It struck her as odd that he'd take the time to pull over at a convenience store.

"And undoubtedly added a shot of brandy to it, as well," Roxy said. "You know those miniature bottles? He keeps a stash in his trunk."

A visibly shaken Coop joined Roxy and Sadie, but didn't sit. He ran his fingers haphazardly through his hair, which made him look even more disheveled. He offered only one brief report before leaving, four words as ominous as the gargoyles that watched.

"This was no accident."

CHAPTER FOUR

"Great coffee," Sadie said as she wrapped her hands around her mug. "Nice and strong, just the way I like it."

"Just the way people need it around here this morning, after what happened last night," Roxy said.

Coop nodded and yawned. The three sat at one of Curtain Call's back tables, away from the front windows where the sun was too bright for their mood. A few stagehands occupied other tables, as well as locals who were café regulars or had gathered to learn more about the shocking news.

"Tell me again why you're sure Brynn's death wasn't an accident," Sadie said to Coop. It had been so late and hectic the night before, that it had been hard for Sadie to follow the details of Coop's explanation. He was also upset and not as coherent as he might normally be.

"Because of the catwalk." Coop pointed up as if he were standing in the theatre. "Brynn obviously fell over the railing to the stage floor."

Roxy frowned. "I find that really odd."

"I'd say odd is an understatement," Sadie said.

"That's not what I mean," Roxy said. "It's odd that anyone would be on the catwalk. We don't even use it in this show."

"Do you think Brynn went up there intending to jump? Do you think she did this to herself?"

Coop shook his head. "No. For one thing, Brynn wasn't like that. She might have been a drama queen and a diva, but she preferred to be the life of the party, if you know what I mean."

"And for another thing?" Sadie asked.

"Before I ran out of there, I noticed that one of Brynn's sleeves was torn, and I swear I saw new bruises on both of her upper arms. They weren't there during the rehearsal."

"Here's a big question, then," Sadie said. What was Brynn doing up on the catwalk after hours?"

"That *is* a big question," Roxy said. "Why *would* she have been there? I saw her leave right after the dress rehearsal finished."

"Obviously, she went back to the theatre," Sadie said. "Maybe she forgot something, a purse, a scarf, a coat?" She turned to Coop. "Can you think of anything out of place in her dressing room, something she might have left behind?"

"No." Coop shook his head. "I can't figure it out. I'm sure no one was in the theatre when I left. I checked every dressing room, restroom, lobby, even the lighting box."

"But — and I'm not accusing, just pointing out a fact, Coop — someone could have slipped into a room you'd already checked while you were checking another. And you did think you might have left the door unlocked," Sadie said. "That would have made it easy for someone to sneak in after you left."

Roxy nodded. "That means two people were inside the theatre at some point after Coop left — Brynn, plus whoever gave her those bruises."

"At least," Sadie said. "You can't rule out the idea that a third person was involved." Sadie had learned long ago that it was best not to narrow down possibilities without facts. Doing so made it easy to overlook potential scenarios.

"It just doesn't make any sense," Roxy said. She stood up and walked over to a self-service area, grabbed a coffee pot from a warming burner, and refilled their mugs. She replaced the pot and returned to the table, sitting down just as the front door opened. Ernie Palmer and Mitchell Morgan walked in, placed an order at the counter, and sat at a table near the back of the café.

"How convenient," Sadie observed. "They're just far enough back to keep us from hearing their conversation."

"That's not unusual," Roxy said. "They never mingle with others. Too full of themselves. Or maybe just preoccupied with the business side of things. I've seen them sit back there many mornings."

When the front door opened again, Sid entered, travel mug in hand. He bypassed the counter without ordering anything, pulled a third chair up to the rear table, and sat down, his back to the rest of the room.

"Now there's a conversation I wouldn't mind hearing," Sadie said. "Producer, publicist, and director, right?"

"Right," Roxy said. "And they've got a lot to discuss quickly if they want to pull off tonight's opening show, starting with calming down the cast. I'd put money on them calling a meeting before noon," Roxy said. She paused as several cast members entered the café. Their expressions ranged from distraught to nonchalant.

"There's Nevada Foster." Coop leaned toward Sadie and pointed discreetly at one of the new arrivals. The slender brunette appeared calm and businesslike as she placed an order at the counter. Collecting her change from the cashier, she strolled to the back of the café and gave Ernie a casual peck on the cheek. After receiving a reassuring hug in exchange, she returned to the counter, picked up her order and sat with the other cast members.

"Nevada's quite attractive, yet not flashy," Sadie noted, turning her attention back to Roxy and Coop. "Even I can see she'll fit that part better than Brynn. No offence meant to the dead," Sadie added hastily.

"Of course she'll fit it better," Roxy said. "Only Sid wanted that larger-than-life bimbo in the lead. Nevada was right for it all along. Ernie never would have backed the show if he'd thought Sid would cast Brynn."

"And Sid wouldn't have cast Brynn if he hadn't been involved with her," Coop added.

"Or if he'd known she was going to dump him once she got the part, right?" Sadie asked.

"Definitely," Coop said. Roxy nodded in agreement.

"It sounds to me like there were plenty of people who might have wanted Brynn out of the way," Sadie remarked. "I'd say the police have their work cut out for them."

"Indeed," Roxy said. "And I'm sure they'll be crawling all over the theatre tonight, watching everyone. Should be quite an evening."

"Attention, everyone!"

The chatter subsided as Sid stood and addressed the crowd. "As you all know by now, there's been a terrible tragedy. The police are still finishing up their inspections, and I've been informed we won't have access to the theatre until approximately 3 p.m. this afternoon. I expect the cast and crew to arrive promptly at 3:15 for an emergency meeting." Sid scanned the room, satisfied when members of the company nodded to acknowledge his orders. "Nevada, you and Russell need to meet as soon as possible to run lines. I know you're prepared, but we've all had a shock, and the more practice you can manage, the better."

"What about the audience?" one crew member asked. "This news is all over the place now. How will they even know the show is still on?" Mumbled comments between others followed.

Sid raised a hand to hush the group. "The box office area has been cleared so Penelope can man the phones. As people call in requesting information or refunds, she'll tell them the show will be going on."

Sadie was quite certain she heard Ernie Palmer mutter "Refunds, as if!" "Sid seems awfully calm in view of the circumstances," she whispered to Roxy. "You know, considering he had been so enamored with Brynn."

"Nah," Roxy said, keeping her voice low. "He's never been one to show emotion, unless someone on the crew misplaces a prop or one of the actors drops a line. Then you'd think the world was on fire. He can get pretty loud."

"She's right," Coop said. "Sid keeps personal stuff to himself. Even when he was seeing Brynn, you could hardly tell from the way he acted."

"Unless it had to do with Russell or Alex, that is," Roxy added.

"What do you mean?" Sadie lifted an eyebrow.

"Jealousy, I suppose." Roxy shrugged her shoulders. "He'd bristle when either one of them — or any man, for that matter — paid too much attention to Brynn. He'd get a strained, annoyed look on his face."

"Sort of like the way he's looking at you now?" Coop suggested. "Since you keep whispering while he's trying to talk?"

"Ha!" Roxy snorted. "He doesn't intimidate me. Besides he's done now. See?" Sid turned back to Ernie and Mitchell, said a quick goodbye, and headed out the door. Others either returned to conversations or finished one more gulp of coffee before departing to prepare for the long day ahead.

Sadie took another sip of her own coffee and set her mug down. "It amazes me that the cast can just get up there on stage and carry on after something this traumatic."

"It's called acting," Roxy said.

"Yes, I can see that." Sadie said. "And I suspect at least one person will be doing an especially brilliant acting job tonight, whether onstage or off."

CHAPTER FIVE

"I don't quite understand it, Coco," Sadie said, directing her comment down toward her tote. Although her habit of talking to her bag in public sometimes drew stares, the scene at The Sea Urchin was lively enough to cover her conversation with the Yorkie. She popped a pretzel in her mouth, and then dropped another into her bag. As always when an edible item happened to fall into the tote, Coco thanked her with a yip. "This whole business of 'the show must go on' seems rather odd to me." Two more pretzels, one more yip.

Sadie glanced at her watch, an old-fashioned face with a wild plastic zebra print band, one of many interchangeable watchbands sold at Flair. It was a customer favorite, both inexpensive and whimsical. A yellow version with a banana print was popular, as was one with purple monkey faces on a lavender background. Another big seller sported dog bones and paw prints. This was Coco's favorite, naturally, but Sadie rarely wore it, as it encouraged Coco to gnaw periodically on Sadie's wrist. The dog's tiny teeth were hardly painful, but it took a certain amount of patience to repeatedly pry them off.

"I thought I'd find you here," Roxy said, sliding into the booth. She kept her jacket on, and shook her head when a passing server asked if she'd like anything.

"You're sure you don't want potato skins, or a drink?" Sadie said. "I'll treat."

"I'm sure," Roxy said. "Well...no, I'm sure. I have to work."

"How'd you escape?" Sadie said. "I figured you'd be tied up with the show until it opened tonight. Which is…" Sadie glanced at her watch again. "Only a couple of hours from now."

"Sid told everyone to take five, and I decided to take twenty. Coop is there if they need something before I get back. Everything's ready to go." Roxy scanned the room. "Hmm, I actually thought I might see Sid down here, fortifying himself with a shot or two before the show. But I'm glad he's not. I'd just as soon talk to you without being interrupted."

"What's up?" Sadie flagged down the server and ordered an apple martini with a lemon twist. As the server walked away, she ate another pretzel and dropped the required counterpart in her bag. *Yip.*

"Word is that the police found something on Brynn's cell phone," Roxy said, glancing at Sadie's tote.

"Her cell phone?" Sadie's ears perked up. Of course, Brynn would have had her cell phone with her. "How did you find that out?"

"From Coop," Roxy said, "who heard it from Penelope."

"The girl in the box office?" Sadie frowned. "What's with that girl's attitude, anyway?"

Roxy shrugged. "Don't ask me. She's been like that since I've known her. Wannabe actress, I guess."

"She resents not being in the show? She wants to be a star, not a ticket seller?"

"I suppose so," Roxy said. "The only time I see her smile is when she's kissing up to Ernie."

"Hmm…" Sadie mulled this over.

"So, like I was saying," Roxy continued, "Coop checked in with her at the box office when he went to see if the police were done inspecting the theatre. Sid sent him there to try to speed things along. She overheard the police discussing evidence they were collecting."

"What else of Brynn's did they find at the scene?"

"Nothing much, as far as I know. A small rhinestone-studded purse, the kind you might use for a night out on the town. I'm guessing the cell phone fell out of that."

"Anything else in there?" Sadie asked.

"Lipstick and a small comb, that's all. And some cash."

"It wasn't a robbery, then," Sadie said. "Not if they left money. It sounds like she was planning a rendezvous," Sadie said. "Lipstick to touch up her makeup, a comb to touch up her hair...do you think she was meeting someone?"

"It sure seems like it," Roxy admitted. "But up on the catwalk? I can't figure that part out. The theatre was empty — or so Brynn would have thought, since it was after hours — so why not just meet in the wings, or her dressing room?"

Sadie's martini arrived, and Roxy reached over as soon as it was delivered. She took a quick sip and set it down. "Thanks," she said. "I have no idea why she'd meet anyone on the catwalk, much less who she would be meeting." She took a second sip of the drink, and then pushed it over to Sadie, as if to offer her some.

"I'll bet the police have an idea by now," Sadie said as she pulled her martini discreetly out of Roxy's reach. "Cell phones hold a lot of information these days."

Roxy nodded. "Sure, contacts and call history..."

"And texts," Sadie added.

"Facebook, Twitter, who knows what sites Brynn kept open," Roxy said. "She was always showy. I can't imagine she'd be secretive with her phone, probably didn't even have password protection on half of it."

"She'd have photos on there, too," Sadie pointed out.

"I'm sure," Roxy said. "Most of them of herself, I'd bet." She grabbed a handful of pretzels, ate one, and then dropped one into Sadie's tote bag. *Yip.* "I'd better get back." Roxy stood. "See you after the show? Come to the stage door. Most everyone will head to Curtain Call, but Coop and I'll need to stay to clean up."

Sadie contemplated the new information as she watched Roxy leave. She'd give a lot to know what was on that cell phone. It certainly sounded like Brynn had been planning to meet someone. Lipstick? Comb? Little rhinestone purse? She had plans, all right. Plans that didn't include lying dead on the stage.

Gulping down the rest of her drink, Sadie left enough money on the table to pay for her martini plus a tip, gathered her tote bag, scooped up two fistfuls of pretzels and headed up to her room. She used her elbow to call the elevator and push the button to her floor. She had to put one fistful of pretzels into her jacket pocket so she could open her door. Once in her room, she switched Coco to her palace and rummaged through the larger than necessary selection of clothes that she'd packed for the trip.

"How about this?" she asked Coco as she stood in front of a full-length mirror and held up the purple mohair sweater and black silk pants that she'd planned to wear. "A little dark? Too funereal in view of the circumstances? Yes, I think so, too." She put them back in the closet and flipped through several other outfits, finally landing on a favorite multi-colored skirt, ivory blouse and teal vest with square gold buttons. Adding earrings to match, she slipped on gold flats and settled into a comfy armchair. She barely had time to open a glossy guide to local attractions when her cell phone rang.

"Hello Roxy," Sadie said. She recognized her friend's number on caller ID.

"Get down to the theatre now," Roxy whispered.

"What for?" Sadie turned a page in the guidebook, landing on an attractive ad for the Monterey Bay Aquarium. She leaned closer to the page as Roxy's next words came through.

"The police are arresting Russell right this minute," Roxy said, still keeping her voice low. Sadie could hear a scuffle and arguing in the background.

"Russell?" Sadie searched her memory for a full name, but couldn't quite recall it with a shark staring her in the eyes.

"Yes," Roxy said. "Russell Garrett, our leading man. They're arresting him for Brynn's murder!"

"So they do think it was murder?" Sadie set the magazine aside and sat up straighter.

"That's what they said when they put the handcuffs on him." Roxy's voice quivered. "Can you come down here?"

"Of course," Sadie said. "I'm not sure how I can help, but I'll be right there."

"Trust me, you can help," Roxy said. "Just get down here. And don't wear anything fancy. Try pants and a sweatshirt. Something dark."

"But…" The line disconnected before Sadie could protest. Sighing, she switched to jeans — at least they had rhinestones on the pockets — and a black sweater. It would have to do.

CHAPTER SIX

The front of the theatre appeared calm as Sadie approached on foot, the hour still too early for the audience to be arriving for the show. But the scene around the side of the building was an entirely different story. The area was abuzz with movement. Cast and crew hovered in clusters, some whispering, some rambunctious, but all upset. Sid stood to the side of the stage door, answering questions from an officer taking notes. Alex and Nevada huddled together, deep in conversation, away from the others, maybe trying to run lines. Coop paced back and forth along the length of the alley, muttering to himself.

Roxy stuck her head out the door just as Sadie arrived. She grabbed her arm and quickly pulled Sadie inside before looking her up and down. Apparently the jeans and long-sleeved sweater met Roxy's approval because she nodded and motioned for Sadie to follow her. It wasn't until they reached a quiet area up the stage stairs, through the wings, and back behind the rear curtain that Sadie began to catch on. When Roxy lifted a headset off a side table and held it out to Sadie, the picture started to become clear.

"You must be kidding," Sadie said.

"I wish I were," Roxy answered. "Please, you have to help me," she pleaded.

"I don't understand," Sadie said. "What about Coop?"

"He can't do his usual job. He has to be in the show now."

Sadie tried to put the pieces together — a challenge between the rustling movement of her tote bag and Roxy's attempts to fit the headset on her. "Because...?"

"Because Alex has to pick up Russell's part."

"Right, because Alex is Russell's understudy," Sadie mumbled, rocking her tote bag as if she were calming a baby. "But what does that have to do with Coop?"

Roxy sighed. "Coop is Alex's understudy."

"I seem to recall buying tickets to this show, you know." Sadie tapped one finger on her chin and looked up at the ceiling. She lowered her eyes quickly at the eerie sight of the roped off catwalk.

"I'll get you a refund, don't worry." Roxy placed the headset on Sadie's head. "I appreciate this, I really do."

"That's so sweet of you," Sadie crooned before flattening her tone. "Considering I haven't the least idea what I'm going to be doing. What about the rest of the crew? Can't one of them step up?"

"They all have specific tasks," Roxy explained. "I need someone who can float. Just follow whatever directions I give through the headset, and you'll be fine. And be prepared for some confusion back here. Nevada and Alex are bound to be nervous, and nerves can be contagious."

"Because they didn't have any warning or rehearsal time?" Sadie asked.

"Right, other than outside in the alley now." Roxy removed Sadie's headset and adjusted it slightly. "Nevada may have expected to fill in for Brynn sometime, and Alex knew he might fill in at some point for Russell. But having both leads out at the same time is exceptionally unusual."

"So Nevada and Alex would never have expected to fill in together," Sadie said, still swinging her arm.

"Not likely." Roxy placed the headset back on Sadie and looked down at the tote bag. "We're going to have to stash your bag somewhere."

Sadie paused. "I can run back to the hotel quickly and get Coco's crate."

Roxy shook her head. "There's no time. You can leave the bag in Russell's dressing room. He obviously won't be using it tonight."

"Won't the police need to check it?"

"They searched every inch of this place earlier today. Whatever it was that made them take Russell in, they already have it." Roxy pulled Sadie aside as two of the stage crew rushed by. "Here, follow me. And watch that your shoulder doesn't bump the back of the curtain. It'll make it ripple."

Roxy showed Sadie to Russell's dressing room and left her to get Coco settled. The small room smelled heavily of cologne and lightly of guilt, a combination that Sadie found unnerving. Still, for lack of a better solution, she set the bag down under the main dressing table. She pulled a collapsible water dish from the tote bag's side pocket and filled it from an accompanying bottle of water. Adding a treat beside the bowl, she gave Coco a short pep talk about being a 'good girl' while she helped a friend. Coco sneezed twice. Sadie closed the door firmly and went in search of further instructions.

The activity backstage began to escalate as cast members returned from the alley to prepare for the show. Nevada and Alex walked the length of the stage, blocking the entrances and exits of their scenes. Sid snapped directions at some of the crew, obviously unsettled by Brynn's death and the police presence. Stagehands adjusted curtains and props. Lights dimmed and brightened, turned red, then yellow, then blue. A voice chirped, "testing, testing," from a sound system overhead. A short woman with a shock of blue hair and a tape measure around her neck steered a wardrobe rack of clothing. As the rack rolled by, Sadie reached out to stroke a particularly appealing jacket in a shade she would label tangerine.

Excluding the detail of the murder, Sadie had to admit the whole excursion had turned into quite the adventure. Here she was, not a spectator, as she had expected to be, but actually in show biz! The feeling was nothing short of exhilarating. She pulled herself up tall and mimed signing an autograph for an eager — albeit invisible — fan. She tilted her head from side to side while accepting accolades from her imaginary admirer. Satisfied that she fit the role nicely, she turned around and found herself face to face with Roxy.

"You're not letting this go to your head, by any chance, are you?" Roxy smirked.

Sadie cleared her throat and squared her shoulders. "Of course not!"

"Good, because we have work to do." Roxy took Sadie's elbow and gave her another tour of backstage, more in depth than before. Not just a scenic tour this time around, she indicated areas for water, towels, and first aid kits. She pointed out electrical cords, glow tape, overhead lights, and a prop table with numerous items: a cane, suitable for an elderly person, a derby hat, a picnic basket with a few pieces of plastic fruit inside. She introduced Sadie to several stagehands. Caught up in the mixed atmosphere of energy and tension, Sadie did her best to memorize everything that Roxy showed her.

"Now," Roxy said. "You'll be able to hear me clearly through the headset. If for any reason you need to take your headset off, you need to say, 'getting off headset' before you do."

Sadie nodded. "And when I put it back on?"

"You'll say, 'back on headset'," Roxy explained. "This way I always know when you can hear me and when you can't. Keep your microphone volume knob down unless I ask you to respond to something. That way noise around you won't leak out to other headsets."

Sadie practiced her two lines as if she were the star of the show. "Getting off headset." "Back on headset." "Getting off headset." "Back on headset."

"Excellent." Roxy said. "You'll also hear me say 'standby' at times. It's important you stay silent when you hear that."

"Got it. And what exactly will you need me to do?" Sadie could barely contain her excitement at this point. She could almost picture the Broadway resume she was building.

"Hopefully nothing." Roxy looked around at the crew. "Everyone knows Coop has to jump in and play Alex's part. They'll each pick up tasks he normally does. And he's only in the first act. He can take over after that."

"Oh." Sadie's spirits dropped. It had all seemed so thrilling a moment before.

"Don't worry," Roxy laughed. "There's always some little thing. Besides, just knowing you're here in case I need an extra hand is enough."

"I don't get an Equity card for this, do I?" Sadie quipped.

"No, you don't." Roxy patted Sadie on the back. "Come with me, let's get you situated somewhere upstage."

"Oh, how lovely!" Sadie began to walk toward the front.

"Um, that means this way," Roxy reached out and caught Sadie's elbow again, turning her around. She guided her to a position in the back, where she'd be out of the way unless needed. Sadie had to admit her designated location was a wise choice. It allowed her to watch both crew and actors move about in preparation without them tripping over her.

The growing activity was intoxicating, as were the muffled sounds of the audience filing in. As she listened to the periodic chatter on the headset, she felt like a true insider. She dutifully kept her volume down and remained quiet, other than responding to one comment: Roxy asking her to make sure she stayed close to the first aid box, towels and masking tape, in case she needed to hand those to anyone. "Roger that!" Sadie responded, not certain it was correct stage lingo, but feeling official, all the same.

"Places!"

Even Sadie knew enough about theatre to stay put when she heard this word. She watched as cast members stepped into positions, and listened as the talk in the auditorium faded away. A deep voice welcomed the audience, and shortly thereafter the show began. Although she could see little from her corner, the back and forth conversation over the headsets fascinated her even if she didn't quite understand it.

"Warning light cue 3"

"Warned."

"Standby light cue 3."

"Standing."

Even the lines the actors delivered intrigued her, as they echoed slightly when they reached Sadie's ears This was quite different from experiencing theatre as part of an audience. Everything she observed and heard carried a spark of newness.

The production itself moved forward. Since she'd attended the dress rehearsal the day before, Sadie knew *Songs to the Sun* to be a light production, but not specifically a comedy. The audience response wavered between silence and light murmurs of appreciation, just as she expected. That is, until the picnic scene just before intermission, when the house suddenly erupted into frenzied laughter. Several stagehands hopped into action, and a sharp command came through the headset, Roxy's voice.

"Sadie, get up here. Now!"

No, it can't be... Sadie hustled to the front, where Roxy waited, a panic-stricken look on her face. Turning toward the stage, Sadie gasped but quickly covered her mouth to silence herself. Center stage, above an open picnic basket, Coco sat on Alex Cassidy's chest, delivering loving kisses to his shocked face.

"Oh, my!" Sadie whispered. "I'll get her." She took a step into the wing, but Roxy pulled her back.

"No, let them improvise this. It's our only hope of a save," Roxy said. "Or at least any chance that Sid won't go ballistic."

It took all of Sadie's willpower to stay put, but she did. And she watched, amazed and grateful, as Nevada jumped right in.

"Oh, Fluffy! I'm so glad you joined us for our picnic," Nevada cooed as she lifted the Yorkie off Alex's chest and pulled an invisible bone from the basket. "We brought treats just in case you showed up."

Fluffy? Really?

It worked. Sadie and Roxy watched as Coco stepped brilliantly into her new role. She licked the hand with the invisible treat, rewarded Nevada with another kiss, and curled up dutifully by her side while Nevada and Alex finished the scene. Only once did she move, trotting confidently back to the picnic basket, hopping in and emerging again with a small bunch of grapes, which she delivered to Nevada as a gift before curling up by her side again. This sweet gesture triggered oohs and aahs from the audience. As the curtain fell for intermission, Sadie and Roxy looked at each other, the same thought running through their minds.

Maybe Sid will spare our lives.

CHAPTER SEVEN

Sadie watched Roxy walk into The Sea Urchin and braced herself for whatever conversation was about to evolve. Coop had caught Coco as soon as the curtain fell for intermission, and he ran into the wings to trade the furry bundle for the headset. Following Roxy's undoubtedly sage advice, she left the theatre as quickly as possible, detouring no more than fifteen seconds to retrieve her empty tote bag from Russell's dressing room on the way out. She had noticed the door was cracked open though she remembered shutting it firmly.

"How bad?" Sadie waited while Roxy took a seat in the cozy booth. Prepared for the worst, she was stunned when Roxy sighed and smiled wearily.

"Not as bad as I expected."

"You're kidding, aren't you?" Sadie said. "You're just trying to make me feel better, when I'm really responsible for ruining opening night."

"Sadie..." Roxy paused to order a draft beer from a server. "You did not ruin the show."

"Well, Coco did. And it's my fault for leaving her unattended in that dressing room. The result was a huge amount of unnecessary drama. I feel terrible." Sadie sipped her martini, her second.

Roxy shook her head. "First of all, Coco...that's her name, right?"

"Yes," Sadie sighed. "Though I wouldn't be surprised if she expects to be called Dame Coco from now on."

43

"Coco's contribution to drama is far upstaged by Brynn's murder and Russell's arrest," Roxy pointed out. "A little comic relief can do us all some good at this point."

"Nice try. I appreciate the sentiment, but I'm sure your director didn't see it that way."

"Actually, he did." Roxy paused as the server slid her beer on the table, and then continued. "I'm sure he was steaming when he first headed backstage. But he sits at the back of the theatre during shows so he can see what the audience sees."

"Well, he saw what they saw, I'm sure." Sadie shook her head, still not quite believing the entire incident.

"Yes, he did. He also heard their reaction. *And* several people stopped him before he got behind the curtain, including Mitchell Morgan."

"Your publicity guy?"

Roxy nodded. "Right. And apparently Mitchell raved on and on about how this was a great stunt to take everyone's minds off the murder. He'd already had one local reviewer pat him on the back and wink."

"That's a good thing?" Sadie popped a pretzel in her mouth. Out of habit, she dropped another on an empty chair beside her, forgetting she had left her tote bag in her hotel room, Coco safely secured in her silk-lined travel crate-AKA-palace, where the crafty canine could contemplate her newly acquired star status without getting into any more mischief.

"Yes, at least Sid thought so, or Sid thought so because Mitchell thought so. Or something like that."

"So your director doesn't want to strangle me?" Sadie tapped a pretzel on the table as she nervously awaited an answer.

"You? Oh, no," Roxy said immediately. "I'm the one in charge of everything that goes on during the show onstage and off. Mishaps are my responsibility, no matter how they happen. It's my job to make sure things run smoothly. I only suggested you leave quickly so you wouldn't get caught in the crossfire."

Sadie's tension began to melt away as she sank back in the booth. "Well, at least I didn't cost you your job. I was worried about that."

"No," Roxy said. "Things go wrong all the time in productions, although…maybe not quite as…unique as Coco's stunt. The important thing is how they're handled. Nevada played right into the unexpected detour. Alex didn't panic — though I found out later he's allergic to dogs — and the crew kept their cool."

"And you stopped me from running out on the stage to get her, when that was my first instinct."

"Yes, we made it work. That's the most important thing. At least, I think so…" Her voice trailed off as her attention moved to the entrance. Sadie followed her gaze, growing alarmed at the sight of Sid Martin and Mitchell Morgan scanning the bar. Both she and Roxy slid down a little lower in the booth, but Sid spotted Roxy, tapped Mitchell's shoulder, and pointed at the women. The two men then made a beeline for the booth as Sadie and Roxy exchanged nervous glances.

"I thought we'd find you here," Sid said, sliding into the circular booth next to Roxy without invitation. "Coop said you'd be meeting your out-of-town friend." Mitchell slid into the opposite side of the booth next to Sadie effectively blocking any possible escape. Her elbow now pressed up against Roxy's, Sadie wasn't sure which made her more nervous: the close quarters, or the anticipation of what was about to happen.

"A scotch on the rocks, please," Sid called to a server a solid ten yards away.

"Make that two," Mitchell echoed.

The server nodded and headed to the bar.

"So, this…"

Mitchell had barely started when Sid interrupted. "So, Roxy, this must be your visiting friend."

Sadie took a deep breath, prepared for the worst. What would it be? Formal apology? Lawsuit? Damages, even? Her mind reeled.

"Yes," Roxy said, her voice far calmer than Sadie expected. Only the guarded look on Roxy's face indicated her friend wasn't sure what the two men were up to. "This is Sadie Kramer, visiting from San Francisco. We've been friends for decades. Sadie, this is Sid Martin, our director, and Mitchell Morgan, our publicist."

"It's very nice to meet you both," Sadie said, not entirely sure this was true.

Sid leaned forward. "We're delighted to meet you, too, Sadie." When he extended his arm, she thought he was going to shake her hand, but he grabbed a bunch of pretzels, instead. "Aren't we, Mitchell?"

Mitchell nodded as he tipped the server for setting the ordered drinks in front of the two men. Both Roxy and Sadie declined an offer from the server to bring them refills, though Sadie suspected they might soon wish they'd ordered another round.

"Indeed we are," Mitchell said, shooting a smile at Sadie befitting a media magician. "And we were wondering how long you plan to be in town. Isn't that right, Sid?"

What a fine-tuned show these two are putting on, Sadie thought. *Time to cut to the chase.*

"So, gentlemen," Sadie said, looking first at one and then the other, "I'm going to save you time by apologizing right now for what happened tonight. This was entirely my fault, not Roxy's..." She held up a hand as Roxy started to jump in. "...And I can't emphasize strongly enough how horrible I feel about it. Coco and I will be leaving first thing in the morning, which is what I'd planned, anyway. So you won't need to worry about any further problems. Again, I am truly sorry."

To her surprise, both men laughed as if she'd just told a doozy of a joke. Sid even reached across the booth and squeezed her hand, a move she found disturbing, if not downright creepy. What was the matter with these men? Roxy rubbed both her temples, eyes closed.

"Tell me this isn't going where I think it's going," Roxy murmured.

"Now, Roxy, just listen" Sid said, reaching for the stage manager's hand. It didn't surprise Sadie in the least to see Roxy pick up her beer quickly and take a gulp, avoiding Sid's grasp. Undoubtedly, this was a manipulative gesture that Roxy had seen many times.

Sid turned his attention from Roxy to Sadie. "We're hoping you might be interested in staying in town."

Roxy cleared her throat. "And I suppose this is where you say, 'and your little dog, too'."

"Nice impression, Rox," Sid said.

Sadie had to agree; Roxy had her Wicked Witch of the North voice down pat.

"Exactly," Mitchell jumped in, beaming.

"Sadie," Sid said, "your little rug rat was the hit of the show."

Sadie bristled. *Rug rat?* "Her name is Coco and she's a Yorkshire terrier."

"Well, then," Sid continued, "your Yorkshire terrier was the highlight of talk during intermission. I'd worried the recent tragedy would be the topic of conversation. But, no, it was all about that little...I mean, your Yorkshire terrier.

"Yes," Mitchell exclaimed. "I even heard one woman say she hoped she could get an autograph on her program after the show."

"Whose autograph?" Sid asked.

"Why, the dog's autograph, of course," Mitchell explained

"Wouldn't that be a *pawtograph?*" Sadie quipped, feeling quite clever, but not expecting anyone to take her seriously. Roxy almost spit out her beer. Sid groaned. But Mitchell's eyes grew wide with delight.

"Yes! Of course it would be! Just think of the marketing angle, the photo opportunities. I can hardly wait to tell Ernie.

He's going to love this." Mitchell jumped up from the table, pulled his cell phone from his pocket, and began pressing numbers furiously into the device.

"Ernie hates dogs," Sid said.

"But Ernie loves money," Mitchell countered, tossing the comment over his shoulder as he headed outside, phone to his ear.

"He has a point there," Sid said, almost to himself, though Sadie and Roxy remained at the table. "And now that his precious Nevada is playing the lead, he'll probably go along with anything." He stood up and downed the rest of his scotch in one gulp. "See you ladies tomorrow."

Sadie watched both men leave the bar before looking at Roxy, puzzled. "Rox, did I somehow miss the part where I agreed to this?"

Roxy sighed. "Apparently, I did, too."

"What does that mean?" Sadie examined the pretzel dish, as if the answer might lie within the salty, twisted dough.

"Don't worry," Roxy said. "It'll get it sorted out in the morning. But, meanwhile...what do you think of their crazy plan?"

"What do *you* think?" Sadie said.

"I think I may have some cue-shuffling to do in the prompt book, that's what I think. I've never had to call 'standby' for a dog before."

"It's not really a normal canine command," Sadie admitted.

"No, it's not. I can barely get humans to follow those directions sometimes. But you still didn't answer my question. What do you think?"

Sadie paused. "I'll have to ask Coco's agent."

Roxy looked almost frightened. "Please tell me your dog does not have an agent."

"Of course not," Sadie laughed. "But it sounded good, didn't it?"

CHAPTER EIGHT

Sadie kicked off her shoes, collapsed onto the hotel bed, and looked at Coco, who was curled up in a serene state of slumber. The Yorkie was oblivious to her newfound fame.

"If you only knew," Sadie whispered.

Coco stirred slightly, stretched her front legs forward and relaxed back into a comfortable sleep, furry head resting on the velvet pillow in her portable palace.

Sadie let her head sink into the luxurious pillowcase on her own bed. What a lovely hotel she'd picked for the weekend, a definite plus to the trip. She wouldn't mind delaying her departure, even just to enjoy the six hundred thread count linens. But how was she going to respond to this wacky turn of events? The show's director and marketing manager simply assumed she'd say OK to their plan. Their enthusiasm had made them forget one little thing: to ask her if she actually agreed. There were logistics to consider, after all. She had her boutique to run, for one thing, though Amber would be perfectly fine running the shop alone. Having a capable assistant manager was the reason she was able to indulge in her adventures.

Like Coco had minutes before, Sadie stretched her arms and legs. She could stay in town without having to make too many arrangements. It would be easy to call or text Amber in the morning, or even pop a quick email her way that night. And, last but certainly not least, there was Coco to consider. That thought made her smile. Coco would be thrilled; she loved being the center of attention. With a few treats as incentive, Sadie was certain she could repeat the performance she'd put on that night. Just recapturing Nevada's attentive pets on the head would do it.

Swinging her legs over the edge of the bed, Sadie reached for the phone and dialed "0" for the front desk. She was greeted by a gracious, professional voice on the other end of the line.

"Yes, Ms. Kramer, how can I help you?" This always surprised her, for some reason. As if the phone itself knew her name. There was no reason this should startle her. She knew perfectly well that the front desk phone displayed the room number and guest name when a call came in.

"I'd like to check your availability," Sadie said. "I'm considering staying in town another night. Is there a chance this room would be open?" She paused, listening to the brief click of a keyboard. "Yes? Oh, how lovely. Go ahead and extend my stay. Thank you so much."

There, that took care of that. Whatever decision she and Coco came to – of course she would discuss it with Coco in the morning – this gave her a reason to linger in Monterey. There was far too much intrigue surrounding Brynn Baker's murder not to see how everything played out. An extra day would provide her with a chance to nose around a bit.

A sudden thought crossed her mind. Could there be a hidden motive behind either Sid or Mitchell's eagerness for Coco's participation in the show, such as diverting attention away from them? She pondered this. Sid could reasonably have had a motive for killing Brynn: anger because of her rejection. Or he could feel she only used him to get the part. Then again, he *had* cast her, so he must have thought she'd be best for the role. Why then would he want her gone? Still, anger was an unpredictable and powerful emotion. It wouldn't be the first time fury drove someone to murder.

Mitchell was a different story. There was no possible motive there, at least not that she could see. Sure, he wanted angles to draw attention to the show, but murder seemed implausible, unless he'd had a personal grievance against

Brynn that Sadie wasn't aware of. That seemed unlikely. Unless...could *he* be the one Brynn had been seeing secretly? Sadie thought this over and ruled it out. Mitchell would have to be a darned good actor himself to keep that hidden from Sid.

A text from Roxy interrupted her contemplation. *Stay. It will be fun.* Sadie smiled. Yes, it would. She tapped back a response. *Fine, but we'll talk about Coco in the morning.* Roxy's turn: *Agreed. Breakfast at 8 a.m. at Curtain Call.*

Sadie put her phone on the bedside table and changed into pajamas. After the wild day, the bright pink flamingo pattern wasn't likely to keep her awake at this point. She guessed right. As soon as she climbed into bed and turned out the lamp, she fell asleep.

* * *

Curtain Call wasn't nearly as crowded as it had been the previous morning. The initial shock of Brynn's murder must have worn off, and Coco's stage debut must not have garnered the same kind of interest. A few solo diners read newspapers and sipped coffee at front window counters. Roxy sat at a table not far from the back wall. Sadie ordered a mocha café and a chocolate croissant, taking a bite before the clerk even handed over her change. How she missed the constant chocolate infusion from Matteo's Cioccolato shop next door to Flair! Juggling her beverage, pastry and tote bag, she joined Roxy.

"You just missed the most interesting conversation," Roxy said. She paused long enough for Sadie to swallow her bite of flaky croissant and prompt her to continue.

"Skip the dramatic effect," Sadie said. "Spill it." She took another bite of croissant and gazed appreciatively at the pastry. *Maybe I should have purchased two...*

"You're not my first companion this morning."

"Let me guess," Sadie said. "Coop?"

"Nope."

"Sid?"

"Wrong again."

"Steven Spielberg."

"Very funny."

"Why?" Sadie smirked. "It wouldn't surprise me if Sid and Mitchell are shopping Coco's movie rights around by now."

Roxy rolled her eyes. "It was Higgins."

Sadie frowned, running the names she knew through her head.

"*Detective* Higgins," Roxy said. "You know, the policeman. Get up to speed, Sadie. Have more coffee, or chocolate, or both."

Excellent idea, Sadie thought. She cruised back to the front and ordered that second croissant. "OK," she said as she settled back down. "What's the story? Why track you down?" Sadie paused suddenly, croissant halfway to her mouth, hoping this was not a bad sign for Roxy. It hadn't occurred to her that Roxy might be a suspect, especially since Russell's arrest. But at this point, maybe Higgins considered everyone at least a "person of interest."

"He wasn't looking for me in particular," Roxy said. "But, as you can see, no one else from the show is here this morning. So I guess I was his only target. Lucky me."

"More information, please," Sadie said. "What was he after?"

"He wanted to know if Russell was in the habit of loaning out his cell phone." Roxy shrugged. "I said I had no idea. I mean, how would I know something like that? I've never borrowed it."

"Any reason why he asked?"

"Apparently, someone sent a text to Brynn's cell phone from Russell's phone, but Russell insists he didn't send it, and he said he lost his phone," Roxy said. "Higgins wanted me to tell him if I'd seen anyone with Russell's phone recently."

"Sounds like he's trying to confirm or rule out Russell's statement," Sadie said. "What did the text say?"

"He wouldn't tell me. I guess that's 'need to know' information." Roxy sipped her coffee and continued. "He also wanted to know if I saw anyone go in or out of Russell's dressing room during the rehearsal that night or earlier that day."

"Did you?"

"No, of course not," Roxy said. "As if I don't have enough to do as it is during a rehearsal. I don't monitor the dressing rooms."

Sadie took another bite of croissant and then paused, pensive. "Who does monitor those rooms? Anyone in particular?"

"Not really. Coop goes in and out sometimes. And Freda, the wardrobe supervisor you saw moving that rack of costumes. And Penelope."

"From the box office?"

"The one and the same," Roxy said. "She cleans the backstage for extra money once or twice a week."

"What about Sid or Mitchell or Ernie, any of the hotshots?"

Roxy shook her head. "Sid's backstage sometimes, but Mitchell and Ernie have no reason to mingle with the lowly company members or do it rarely. When they come by, they usually stick to the lobby, or sit in the back of the auditorium itself. Ernie only comes backstage to pick Nevada up from rehearsals or to bring her coffee. Mitchell doesn't hang around any part of the theatre very often. He's usually just running around town working on publicity. Unless..." Roxy stopped talking and sighed.

"Unless what?"

Roxy pointed over Sadie's shoulder. "Unless he's chasing us down."

Sadie turned toward the door and saw Mitchell entering. He plastered a wide smile across his face at the sight of the two women. Raising a finger to signal he'd be right there, he placed an order at the counter. Within sixty seconds, he was seated at the table.

"So, I have posters in the works, called in a favor with the local printers. We can have Coco's photo dropped in later today before they print. I'll need a headshot for the lobby – she has one, right?" Sadie opened her mouth, but Mitchell didn't pause. "We'll do an insert in the programs – no way to reprint those. And...what, Roxy?"

"For one thing," Roxy said, "have you considered saying good morning to us?"

"Good morning." Mitchell's words came out semi-garbled as he took a huge bite of his muffin at the same time he spoke. He took a gulp of coffee to wash the bite down then uttered a few choice expletives once he realized how hot the coffee was.

"And for another thing," Roxy continued, "you never asked Sadie if putting Coco in the show would be OK."

"What?" Mitchell looked shocked. "What are you talking about? We all agreed last night." His expression turned immediately to panic. He turned to face Sadie directly. "You can't back out now, Ms..."

"Kramer," Sadie said, not sure whether to be amused or annoyed that he'd already forgotten her name. After all, she *was* the new leading lady's manager. "But 'Sadie' is fine."

"All right, Sadie it is." Mitchell grinned as if the two had just sealed the deal.

"Mitchell," Roxy interrupted. "The only two people who decided this last night were you and Sid. You'd better ask Sadie. It's up to her."

A sudden, insistent yip emerged from the tote bag. Mitchell looked at the bag and raised an eyebrow.

"It's actually not entirely up to me," Sadie said. She broke off a tiny piece of croissant and dropped it into the tote. "Ask your potential star."

"She's not serious, right?" Mitchell said to Roxy.

"Sounds serious to me," Roxy said, rocking back in her chair.

To his dismay, Sadie picked up the tote and set it in Mitchell's lap. He gazed down into the bag and frowned. "You don't really expect me to talk to him, do you?"

"Her," Sadie corrected. "And Coco is very much her own dog. I'd ask if I were you."

"Go on, Mitchell." Roxy egged him on. "You do want this, don't you?"

"Yes, of course." Mitchell hesitated, and then looked over his shoulder.

"No one's watching you," Roxy said. "Go ahead, ask."

Mitchell shook his head, and then leaned over the bag, reluctantly. "How would you like to be a star, you little..."

"Yorkshire terrier," Sadie filled in. "Her name is Coco."

"Probably Ms. Coco to you," Roxy added.

Mitchell looked back up, rolled his eyes and, as if dared, leaned forward and addressed the bag again. "Would you like to be a star, Ms. Coco?" In a split second, Coco jumped up, paws flopped over the edge of the bag, and licked Mitchell's face.

Sadie laughed, certain that Mitchell's expression was the oddest mix of a cringe and a smile that Sadie would ever see.

CHAPTER NINE

Sadie and Roxy stood in the wings and watched the commotion. Coco sat patiently center stage inside an open picnic basket, head swiveling each time she heard her name from one direction or another.

"I've never re-blocked a scene to incorporate a dog before," Sid said as he paced. "This is highly unusual." He ran one hand through his hair and shot a look in Roxy and Sadie's direction, as if they were to blame.

"Should I remind him this wasn't my idea?" Roxy whispered to Sadie.

"Nor mine," Sadie whispered back.

The cast of the picnic scene stood around, half irritated that they'd been called in for an emergency rehearsal, and half amused by the circumstances.

"If this were film, at least we'd have an animal trainer here to help out!" Sid exclaimed. This time he glared at Mitchell and Ernie, who sat in the front row of the theatre. Mitchell plastered on an encouraging smile, while Ernie simply gazed lovingly at the stage. Even from her position to the side, Sadie could almost see dollar signs gleaming in his eyes. She understood why. Not only did the producer finally have his favorite girl in the lead, he had seen ticket sales soar as the word got out about the unusual cast addition.

"Any suggestions, Roxy? Anyone?" Sid turned around in a circle, arms out to the sides.

"I'm not supposed to answer that, am I?" Sadie whispered.

Roxy shrugged. "I don't know anymore. He looks pretty desperate to me. I'd say all bets are off."

"I don't suppose he could get upset at me," Sadie mused. "If I leave, Coco leaves."

"Good point," Roxy said. "Though not a good idea after those papers you signed today."

Sadie sighed. It was true. She'd been amazed how lickety-split the show's lawyer had sent over a contract for her signature. Not that she was dismayed, by any means. It had never occurred to her that Coco would get paid, and a pretty sum, at that. Enough for a trip to Palm Springs after the show ended, or New York, or New Orleans. Not quite enough to head off to Paris or London, at least not unless the show picked up the option on Coco's contract and extended the production.

The option part had been confusing to Sadie at first, especially the fact the option was in the producer's control, not for Coco herself (or Sadie as her manager) to decide. After all, Coco was their new star. The potential deal-breaker became a non-issue, however, once Sadie was able to negotiate a child-sized director's chair with Coco's name on it, as well as unlimited supply of chocolate lava cake for herself.

"I have a suggestion," Sadie said. Sparkles of light glinted off her sleeve as she waved her arm at Sid. The black, long-sleeved blouse with wrist to shoulder rhinestones that she'd found at a local shop after breakfast had seemed the right combination of backstage frump fashion and stage mom couture. Granted, her position mostly consisted of monitoring the first aid kit and keeping Coco out of trouble now. But it was only right to dress the part.

"Yes?" Sid fought against a frown as muffled laughter echoed across the stage.

Sadie took a step forward, and then paused, looking at Roxy for permission.

"Why not? I think anything goes at this point." Roxy extended an arm toward the stage.

"I think," Sadie started and then paused, looking out into the theatre. She raised one glittering arm and shielded her eyes, momentarily forgetting why she'd even walked out onto the stage. "Wow, those lights are bright!" Another wave of soft laughter floated through the air. "How can you guys even see? Oh, I guess you can't." Sadie took a couple of steps toward the front of the stage, her eyes looking straight out into the auditorium, intrigued. Aside from Ernie and Mitchell, in the center of the front row, and two women to one side, she couldn't see anything.

"Stop!" Roxy jumped out and grabbed Sadie's arm, pulling her back. "You can't go past that tape." She pointed to a line on the floor. "That marks the edge of the stage."

"Well!" Sadie exclaimed, moving back and putting her hands on her hips. "That's just downright dangerous! Aren't you all afraid of getting hurt?" She shook her head. "My, oh, my."

Sid glanced at his watch. "You said you had a suggestion?" Crossing his arms, he began to tap his foot.

Sadie looked back at Roxy, who had started tapping her own watch. Even Coco barked from her picnic basket, urging Sadie to hurry up.

"I don't think you need to re-bolt anything," Sadie said.

"Block," Roxy whispered. "Re-block."

"Right," Sadie said, correcting herself. "Re-block, that's what I meant. Everything is blocky enough." This elicited more laughter, not at all muffled this time.

"I'm not sure 'blocky' is even a word," Sid said. "It's certainly not theatre terminology."

"I kind of like it," one cast member murmured, eliciting another round of laughter.

Sid clapped his hands sharply. "Everyone, we don't have time for this. Save your shenanigans for the cast party."

"Oh! A party!" Sadie exclaimed. "I just love a good party!" She looked around smiling, then became serious when no one responded. Clearing her throat, she got down to business. "OK, I don't know much about theatre, aside from when Roxy and I starred in our third-grade production of Annie."

"One line each..." Roxy whispered.

"But I wouldn't change anything," Sadie said. "Your audience liked it just the way it was last night. Isn't that why you asked Coco to stay?"

"That's true," a loud voice echoed from the front row of the theatre. "That's the reason Coco is here."

"Yes, Ernie." Sid sighed and leveled his eyes on Sadie. "That's the reason *Coco* is here."

"Well," Sadie said, ignoring the director's insinuation that her own presence was unnecessary, "then don't change anything. Coco is going to do whatever she's going to do."

"True." a young man in picnic attire piped up. "You can't teach an..."

Sadie glowered at the actor, who interrupted himself mid-sentence.

"...A beautiful dog new tricks, I was going to say."

"That's exactly right," Sadie said. "Though, come to think of it..."

"What? Quickly, please." Sid tilted his head to the side, impatient.

Sadie looked at Coco, who tilted her head to the side, as well.

"We have an old trick that might work," Sadie said. "Now that I think about it, I can see why she gave Nevada the grapes last night." She looked at Coco. "Give toys, Coco." Obediently, Coco ducked down into the picnic basket and popped up with the grapes from the previous night. Jumping out, she trotted over to Nevada and delivered them, just as she had before. She received a pet on the head from Nevada, and then returned to the picnic basket.

Again, Sadie gave the command. "Give toys." Coco emerged with a plastic banana, which she dragged over the edge of the basket and across the floor, choosing Alex as the recipient this time. The cast members applauded. Now, enthusiastic from the responses, she trotted confidently back to the basket, chose another item, and delivered it to yet another person.

Sadie looked over at Roxy. "Is there any way she could hear me give the commands?"

"I think I can arrange that," Coop said. "I can set up a small speaker inside the picnic basket."

She turned her gaze back to Sid. "You see? It will be fine."

"OK, nothing else changes, then," Sid said. "Nevada and Alex, you two will adlib that final scene, like last night." Sid clapped his hands again. "You can all go. Call time is 6. I expect everyone here promptly."

CHAPTER TEN

Coco sat demurely in front of the dressing room mirror.

"Isn't she adorable?" Sadie squealed. "I just love the new look!"

Coco tipped her head to the side and wagged her tail, admiring herself in the mirror. The flashy rhinestone collar and six-inch wide sequined bow framed the Yorkie's head well, though it also dwarfed it. The matching three-inch sequined bow on her tail completed the look. Sadie had to hand it to the wardrobe girl for the inventive accessories.

"I debated a small tutu, but ruled it out," Freda said. She snipped a thread off the larger bow and let go of the small pair of scissors strung on a ribbon around her neck.

Sadie almost choked on a forkful of chocolate lava cake. "Oh, it's a good thing you did!" she exclaimed. "Coco is terrified of tutus!"

"Afraid of tutus?" Roxy looked up from her prompt book, where she was marking a new lighting cue to spotlight the picnic basket. "Is that a real thing? A fear of tutus?"

"I suppose it could be," Sadie mused. "Tutuphobia, maybe?"

"A canine disorder?" Roxy quipped, going back to writing her notes. "Then again…" She looked back up. "I may have had that as a child. But I think it might have been Preferring Soccer to Ballet Syndrome, instead."

"Why?" Freda asked.

"I was just always a tomboy at heart," Roxy said, assuming the question was for her.

"No, I meant, why is this dog afraid of tutus?"

Sadie laughed. "Well that's a funny story. A few years ago, there was a Halloween carnival at a nearby dog park. Costumes were encouraged. So, I figured, why not?"

"You put her in a tutu?" Roxy asked. "Made her into a Yorkie Prima Ballerina?"

"Heavens, no, nothing that crazy." Sadie shook her head. "Coco was dressed up as Carmen Miranda."

"Right…" Roxy said slowly. "Because that is less crazy than being a ballerina."

Sadie huffed. "Well, to Coco it certainly was. She's always been fond of salsa music, so I figured a Brazilian twist could work."

"How did that go?" Roxy asked.

"Fine," Sadie said. "After a few days of me singing "The Dog from Ipanema" to her, she fell right into the role. Even developed some four-pawed bossa nova moves." Sadie smiled proudly while Roxy and Freda exchanged looks. "And she adored the headpiece I made for her," Sadie added. "It had perfectly balanced miniature pieces of fruit, held securely in place with an elastic chin strap."

"Hence her fascination with the fruit in the picnic basket," Roxy said.

Sadie's eyes opened wide. "It hadn't occurred to me, but I guess so!"

"I'm having trouble tying this in with her fear of tutus, for some reason," Freda said.

"Ah, I'm getting to that." Sadie began to pace, giving the story a dramatic tone. "There was another dog there, a Poodle named Precious Princess, I believe, who was decked out in full *Swan Lake* regalia."

"White or black?" Freda asked.

"Fur or tutu?" Sadie said.

Freda sighed. "Tutu, of course."

"Black," Sadie said.

"That's explains it," Freda said. "Odile. I'd be afraid, too."

"I could not be more confused about where this conversation is going," Sadie said, rhinestones shimmering as she stopped pacing and placed her hands on her hips.

"On a tangent, I dare say." Roxy sent a disapproving look in Freda's direction. She then turned to Sadie. "Odile is the Black Swan in Swan Lake, the evil daughter of the evil sorcerer Von Rothbart. Had the girl worn white ..."

"Poodle," Sadie corrected.

"Of course." Roxy sighed. "Had the poodle worn white, she would have been Odette, the Swan Princess."

"You must have seen the Black Swan costume that Margot Fonteyn wore opposite Nureyev in 1964, right? Magnificent." Freda looked past Sadie to Roxy.

"How old do you think I am, Freda?" Roxy snorted.

"That gold braiding and sequins, the lace and pearls..." Freda continued. "I saw it in a book once."

Sadie cleared her throat. "*SO*, it turned out Precious Princess was not so precious. She became enamored of the fruit that I'd so carefully positioned on Coco's headpiece. She chased my poor dog all over that park, pulling fruit off her head. She was too quick for her owner and me to catch her at first. Poor Coco was terrified, and she hid behind benches and trash cans. It was traumatizing. She only calmed down when I collected the fruit, took her home, and reassembled her costume. Since then, she panics anytime she sees a tutu."

"I take it you two don't go to the ballet," Roxy said.

"Heavens, no!" Sadie covered Coco's ears, as if the mere reference might send the Yorkie into a panic.

"Watch that bow!" Freda snapped, pointing to the sequined piece atop Coco's head.

Coop peered into the room. "Am I interrupting anything important?"

"Hardly," Roxy said.

"Good," Coop replied. "Sid wants to see you up front, Rox."

"Fine, tell him I'll be right there." She turned back as Coop left. "Freda, are we done with Coco's wardrobe fitting?"

"As done as we'll ever be." Freda removed the collar and bows, placing them neatly on the dressing table, where they could be put on just before the show. Coco whined slightly as the wardrobe manager left the room, as if she were sorry to lose both the attention and the flashy getup.

"I've got to go see what Sid wants," Roxy said. "You two are free to go. Call time is six o'clock."

"Fine, I'll have my phone with me," Sadie said as she picked up Coco and placed her in her tote bag.

"That means you need to be here at six o'clock," Roxy clarified.

"Oh." Sadie paused, thinking back to Sid's words when he dismissed the cast. "Got it."

* * *

The hotel lobby was quiet when Sadie entered. It was the lull between when guests checked out in the morning and new guests checked in during the late afternoon or evening. A dull hum of voices wafted out from The Sea Urchin, which appeared empty at first glance. The room wasn't empty, though. At the far end of the bar sat a man who resembled the lead actor in *Songs to the Sun*. Was this possible? Wasn't he in jail?

Since she hadn't officially met Russell yet, Sadie took advantage of her anonymity to slink casually inside. She sat at a table far enough away to avoid arousing suspicion, but close enough to eavesdrop on the animated conversation Russell was having with the bartender. She set her tote bag on the chair beside her and debated drink options as a server approached.

"What can I get for you?"

"Just coffee would be great," Sadie said. It was bound to be a long evening. Staying awake and thinking clearly would be wise. "And more pretzels, if you don't mind."

"Coffee it is," the server said. "And I'll refill the snack dish."

"Thank you," Sadie said, and then leaned closer and whispered. "Isn't that one of the actors from the show? You know, from the theatre down the street?"

"Yes." The server nodded as she placed a napkin on the table in front of Sadie and picked up the half-empty bowl of pretzels. "You know they took him down to the jail?"

"Really?" Sadie raised her eyebrows. "Why?"

"I guess they took him in for questioning. Something to do with the other night," the server said, keeping her voice low. "You know another star in that show died, fell from the theatre's catwalk. At least that's what they said on the news."

"I heard something about that," Sadie said, grabbing a few pretzels as the dish hovered in the air. More room for refills. "Well, I can understand relaxing here after an ordeal like that," Sadie said.

"Oh, he's here all the time. He's sort of friends with Tony, our bartender." She tipped her head in the direction of the sandy-haired man behind the bar who was pouring a drink for Russell.

"Will he be performing tonight?" Sadie asked suddenly, concerned Coco was about to lose her newly found star status.

"I certainly hope not," the server whispered. "He's on his fourth scotch, I think. I'll get your coffee."

Sadie settled back as the server retreated to the bar and poured coffee from a glass carafe. Once the coffee and full bowl of pretzels were in front of her, Sadie dropped a pretzel into the tote bag and turned her attention to the conversation at the bar.

"I can't believe Ernie left me in there overnight." Russell's voice sounded shaky compared to the smooth voice Sadie heard coming from the stage the night of the dress rehearsal. The muted acoustics of the bar were far different from the bold echo in the theatre. The scotch probably wasn't helping, either.

"Be grateful he showed up to bail you out at all. You're lucky," the bartender said. "You said the text on the victim's phone was from you?"

"Yes, but that makes no sense, Tony. I didn't even have my phone that night. I couldn't find it after the dress rehearsal."

"You think someone took it?"

"What else could it be?" Russell said. "Someone's trying to set me up."

"Anyone in the cast have jealousy issues?" Sadie thought Tony sounded more like a bartender making idle conversation than a friend who was genuinely curious or concerned.

"Of Brynn? Sure," Russell said. "Nevada, for one, though she never let on. But she knew she should have had Brynn's part."

"Nevada is the understudy, right?"

"Right. So now she *is* playing the lead."

"With you." Running water and a clink of glasses indicated Tony was washing out barware while talking. "She's playing opposite you now."

"Yes," Russell said. "Though not tonight. Sid told me to wait until next weekend to come back. They have some stupid dog in the show tonight."

Sadie bristled, hoping Coco hadn't heard the rude comment. Looking into the tote bag, she was pleased to see Coco curled up in a ball, snoozing.

"Ah, yes," Tony laughed. "I heard about that. Publicity stunt, I guess."

"That's what I'm figuring," Russell said. "Or diversion tactic. I wouldn't put it past Mitchell to come up with a crazy scheme like that. But I can use the night off after everything that's I've been through. I didn't sleep too well last night, either."

"No, I bet you didn't." More clinking of glasses.

"I just can't figure out why someone would want to frame me," Russell continued, his words a touch slurred. "Or how they got ahold of my phone. Without me knowing, even. I always have it with me."

"Always?"

"Yes!" Russell insisted, his voice louder than before. "Except…" He paused. "Except occasionally I leave it in the car."

"Do you keep your car unlocked?"

"Never unlocked."

"Anyone borrow your car recently?"

"Absolutely not."

"Where else?"

"Nowhere." The conversation paused, and then Russell spoke again. "Wait, that's not true. I don't take it on stage with me."

"What do you do with it?"

"I leave it in my dressing room."

"Do you lock the door?"

"No, I don't lock it. I don't need to. No one goes into my dressing room."

That you know of, Sadie thought to herself. *An unlocked door is an unlocked door.*

Russell stood up, downed the rest of his drink, and set the glass down on the bar counter with a solid clunk. "I'm out of here. Where's my car key?"

"You can pick it up tomorrow, Russell. I'll call you a cab."

Russell grumbled. "First I lose my phone, now my key. Fine, I'll walk. Half a mile. No problem."

Sadie lowered her head and sipped coffee as Russell walked out. From the corner of her eye she could see the bartender shaking his head. Gathering up her tote bag, she left money on the table for coffee and a tip, and headed to her room. Coco's idea of a short nap suddenly sounded appealing. It was going to be a long night.

CHAPTER ELEVEN

When the alarm beeped, Sadie sat up and checked the clock. 4:30 p.m. She had just the right amount of time to dress, have a quick bite at Curtain Call, and get to the theatre on time. She prepared a bowl of Coco's current favorite food. Sadie alternated, as some days Coco wanted her kibble mixed with a petite can of filet-mignon-flavored fare, while other days she preferred fresh grilled chicken strips with a touch of gravy. The canned food was much more practical when traveling, so on this particular night Sadie poured the kibble/filet mignon mixture into Coco's Villeroy and Boch china food dish, and then jumped in the shower.

Thirty minutes later, Sadie had donned a second black outfit that she'd found at the mall. After all, there was no reason to buy just one set of clothes when one could buy two. She loved the neckline on this outfit, its gold-beaded trim. It wasn't as flashy as the rhinestone top she'd worn to the emergency rehearsal, but would be just right in view of Roxy's subtle suggestion that she wear something less sparkly. Satisfied she looked every bit the proud stage mom that she was, she put away Coco's dinner bowl, washed Coco's paws and brushed both her hair and the pup's fur, and walked down to Curtain Call.

The café was busier than she expected it to be at this time. At only a few minutes past five o'clock, half of the tables were already occupied, as well as several counter seats along the front window. Sadie waited in a short line, ordered a ham and cheddar croissant and an iced tea, and sat at a miniscule table against the wall. She pulled the only other chair around from the opposite side of the table and set down the tote bag. She settled in to people watch as she sipped her iced tea.

She didn't know most of the diners, though she recognized a couple of crew members – none with a name she could place. She continued to scan the room as April, the cashier from the first day Sadie had arrived in town, slid the warm croissant in front of her. She thanked April for the food and paused to look around the room again as the girl stepped away. That was when she noticed two women in a far corner, hunched together in animated conversation. *Penelope and Freda?*

"This is interesting, Coco," she said, leaning over the tote and dropping a crumb of croissant in at the same time. "These two seem like an odd duo. I wouldn't have guessed that they knew each other more than in passing if at all since they work completely different parts of the theatre. But from the looks of things, they know each other well."

Over the years, Sadie had made an amateur study of the ways people behaved during conversations. Casual acquaintances exhibited different body language and gestures from close friends during intense discussions. She could also tell if people were talking about business or about more personal topics. Penelope and Freda acted like good friends. Sadie imagined they were gossiping based on how they cupped their hands around their mouths and turned away from other customers' direct view. Even if she'd mastered lip-reading – which she hadn't, though she always thought it would come in handy – she wouldn't have been able to pick up the conversation. Still, body language revealed a lot. And Penelope and Freda's told her something was going on.

"Deep in thought?"

The voice startled Sadie. She looked up to see Roxy standing beside her, a paper bag in one hand and a coffee cup in the other.

"I didn't see you come in."

"Dinner," Roxy said, lifting both arms in the air. "I ordered to go at the counter. Chicken fingers and fries. Not healthy, I know, so guilty as charged. But I don't have time to sit down to eat. I might get to nibble backstage before it gets busy."

"Smart," Sadie said. "I might trade you some chocolate lava cake for a few fries."

"Deal," Roxy said, reaching forward with the paper bag so Sadie could reach in. "So, what were you so deep in thought about?"

As she bit into a French fry, she nodded toward Penelope and Freda in the far corner.

"Oh, those two," Roxy said. "They're always gossiping about something."

"They look pretty close. Their friendship seemed strange to me since they work at such different jobs." Sadie reached into Roxy's bag and pulled out a few more fries.

"Thick as theatre thieves," Roxy said. "Freda's the one who got Penelope the job in the box office. They worked together before, not sure where. Down in L.A., maybe. Or San Diego."

"I wonder if they know anything about what happened the other night." Sadie watched the two women, still huddled together in conversation. "Did Detective Higgins question them?"

"No idea," Roxy said. "He might have. He was at the theatre just after that picnic scene rehearsal, asking questions. Freda was there then." Roxy offered her paper bag to Sadie one more time and then rolled the top back up. "It wouldn't surprise me if they knew something. Freda sees everything that goes on backstage, and Penelope sees what goes on up front."

"So, between the two of them..."

Roxy shrugged. "He might have questioned Freda today, but Penelope wasn't around. She comes in just before the box office opens."

"Unless she's cleaning," Sadie said. "You said she cleans backstage once or twice a week."

"Right, she does."

"Do you know the last time she cleaned?"

Roxy frowned. "That's a good question. Let me look at the schedule. I know the theatre was cleaned the night before the dress rehearsal, but we have a cleaning service that comes in once each week, as well, to do a more professional job. I don't know who was on that night."

"I'd be curious to know," Sadie said.

"So would I, now that you mention it." Roxy peeked into the tote bag. "I've got to get back. See you and the little star at six."

"We'll be there," Sadie said. She watched Roxy leave and then looked back at the far table. Freda and Penelope were gathering their belongings and standing to leave. The two were now silent, their faces blank, as if gossiping had exhausted all emotion. They left the café without speaking to each other again and turned toward the theatre.

"What do you think, Coco?" Coco yipped as Sadie finished off the croissant. "I agree, something is off with those two." Taking another sip of iced tea, she glanced at her watch, admiring the black strap with gold musical notes. Yet another favorite from her boutique's selection of fashion watchbands, this one matched the gold beaded trim of her blouse, as well as dangling gold earrings in the shapes of treble and bass clefs. "Time to go, Coco."

Sadie headed to the theatre, eyes widening as she passed the box office. A flyer with the words "Special Appearance" and Coco's picture flanked the regular production poster. Inside the ticket window, Penelope worked at the counter, sorting envelopes that Sadie assumed to be will-call tickets. Roxy had mentioned the phone lines had been swamped with calls from eager theatregoers who hoped to see the show. Penelope looked up at Sadie without a smile, and then immediately went back to work.

Identical flyers had been posted on each side of the theatre entrance, framed in ornate gold-brushed wood, a style reminiscent of museum pieces. Mitchell had certainly pulled some fast action from the local print and frame shops.

Peering through the glass panes inlaid in the heavy doors, Sadie could make out a linen-covered table with a stack of what appeared to be programs on it. The bold sign behind it read "Pawtographs" in a Broadway-type font, black and red ink printing surrounded by stylish paw prints. *Impressive*, Sadie thought.

Rounding the corner of the theatre, Sadie bustled down the side alley to the stage door, where a frazzled-looking Coop greeted her.

"Roxy needs you backstage as soon as possible."

Sadie looked at her watch. "We're not late, right? Roxy said to call at six."

"To call? Oh, never mind, I get it," Coop said. "No, you're not late. Go on back. She'll meet you in Russell's dressing room. That is, Coco's dressing room for tonight. I'll be in to explain how the speaker in the picnic basket will work."

"Oh!" Sadie exclaimed. "Wonderful! You got that set up!" She looked down into the tote bag, "Did you hear that, Coco? You have your own speaker now!" Sadie looked back up at Coop as a yip of approval emerged from the tote. "How will she hear me? Will I have a microphone?"

"I hope not," Sid muttered as he walked by. Sadie frowned at the director's back.

"Ignore him," Coop said. "He's stressed because Higgins has been hanging around. I'll give you a headset. Don't worry, it will be easy."

Sadie thanked Coop and made her way back to the dressing room, where she found Roxy pacing, head down in her prompt book. She appeared almost as frazzled as Coop had seemed when she met him at the stage door.

"Oh, good. I'm glad you're here."

"We're not late, you know." Sadie sighed, slightly irked at pointing this out again. "The call time was six o'clock." She mentally patted herself on the back for sounding like a pro. She could get into this theatre thing if she stuck around. She was already getting the lingo down. "You know, Rox, everyone seems tense tonight. Coop looked semi-frantic, and Sid snapped at us for no reason."

Roxy closed the prompt book and set it on the edge of the dressing table. "It's just that Higgins is hanging around."

"That's what Coop said."

Roxy sighed. "It wouldn't be a big deal, but his timing is bad. He's questioning cast members as they arrive, which shakes people up and takes their focus away from the show."

"Well, he has a right to question people," Sadie pointed out. She put the tote bag down and lifted Coco out, setting the Yorkie on the dressing table. Coco proceeded immediately to admire herself in the mirror, licking one paw and patting down a patch of wayward fur behind one ear.

"True," Roxy sighed. "And he does have a warrant *and* he bought a ticket to tonight's show, so we just have to deal with having him here. Sid's not happy about it, but there's nothing he can do. Same thing goes for Ernie and Mitchell, who are also peeved."

"Ah, the big shots are here, too. Did you hear that, Coco?" Sadie looked at Coco, who was now licking Roxy's prompt book. Roxy picked up the book and, hesitating briefly, finally shrugged her shoulders and tucked it under her arm.

"Yes, they're here," Roxy said. "Much to Higgins' delight, I might add. He spent a good fifteen minutes grilling Ernie, from what I heard."

"Ernie?" Sadie said. "That's interesting. Ernie doesn't have much to do with the show, at least in terms of hands-on activity."

"True, but he's got money behind it, and he didn't expect Brynn to get the lead, as you know."

Sadie nodded. "I remember that from overhearing the conversation the first day I was in town. "He wanted Nevada to play the lead, only invested in the show because he thought she would get it."

"And now she has it," Roxy pointed out. "Just like he wanted originally."

"So he had two things to gain from Brynn being out of the way," Sadie said. She sat down in front of the dressing table and lifted Coco into her lap. "Nevada got the lead part, and he saved himself from a financial disaster, at least from his perspective. He was able to kill two birds with one catwalk."

Roxy stared at Sadie. "There are so many things wrong with that metaphor that I don't even know where to start."

"Well, you know what I meant," Sadie said, brushing the comment off. "He had motives for killing Brynn."

"I suppose, but so did other people. And I'm not sure Ernie even knows how to get up to the catwalk. Besides, even with Brynn as the lead instead of Nevada, the play was doing all right financially. And all Ernie really cares about is money. Look, I have to go check with the lighting technicians about the new cue for Coco's spotlight. Sit tight. Freda will be here soon to dress Coco, and Coop will stop by to explain the picnic basket speaker."

Both Freda and Coop showed up within minutes. Freda set to work brushing Coco's fur and attaching the rhinestone collar and sequined bows securely.

Coop brought the picnic basket in and demonstrated how Sadie should use the headset to give Coco her commands. After the practice run went well enough that Coco grabbed the brush from Freda's hand, hopped off the dressing table, and presented the brush to a crew member in the hallway, Sadie and Coop both stepped outside, leaving Freda and Coco to finish up without any wayward commands disrupting them.

"I see Coco takes her role seriously," Coop said as he adjusted the headset on Sadie,

"Yes, she does," Sadie said proudly. "Testing, testing," she said into her microphone. She beamed at Coop. "I've always wanted to do that."

Coop laughed. "Between your willingness and Coco's determination, I'm sure the picnic scene will be in good hands. And paws," he added.

"It had better be," Sid said, passing by again. He looked no less disgruntled than before.

"Sheesh," Sadie said once the director moved on. "He's in a mood tonight, isn't he?"

Coop nodded. "Understandably so. His job is on the line. Ernie's watching him. New critics are in the audience tonight. And apparently he and Russell had an altercation earlier because Sid didn't want Russell in the show tonight. He's out of jail."

"Yes, I know." Sadie said. "I saw him at The Sea Urchin this afternoon."

"Figures," Roxy said, joining the two of them. "That's where he heads to drown his sorrows. He must have been pretty upset about not being in the show tonight."

"I'd say he sounded far more upset about being accused of sending Brynn a text. Claims someone else borrowed or stole the phone to frame him." Sadie did her best to recall the details she'd picked up between Russell's conversation with the bartender and the server's gossipy additions.

Freda emerged from the dressing room, leaving the door open, and headed down the hallway, scissors swinging as she went. "She's all yours," she called over her shoulder.

"Thanks," Sadie said. She watched as Roxy and Coop took off to handle other aspects of show preparation, and then retired into the dressing room to sit with Coco. Even with wardrobe out of the way, and directions for the new speaker in the picnic basket, she couldn't help but feel the evening was going to follow its own, unpredictable course.

CHAPTER TWELVE

From the wings, Sadie could hear an active buzz coming from the theatre, louder than it had been the night before.

"Sounds busy out there," she said to Roxy, who stood nearby.

"Sold out," Roxy said, lifting a finger to caution Sadie not to talk while she spoke into her headset. "Is that picnic basket ready? All props inside for Coco to give out?" At the response, she nodded. "Thanks, Coop." She turned to Sadie. "All set. The basket has one item for each person in that scene. All small enough for Coco to carry."

"Great!" Sadie said, her energy growing. She stood tall, looking out at the stage as if it were an Academy Awards platform.

She turned when someone tapped her arm. Mitchell stood behind her, a stack of programs in his hands and big smile on his face.

"We have a table set up in the lobby for Coco to sign autographs after the show."

"I think you mean *Pawtographs*," Sadie quipped. After all, it was only fair to get the details right. Besides, she'd already seen the sign.

"Yes, of course," Mitchell said. He opened the front of a program on top of the stack and pointed to an empty space. "This is where the dog should sign, er...print, er...paw. Whatever. There's an ink pad there and a blotter."

Roxy turned toward Mitchell, annoyed. "Do you really have to explain this right now, right here? We're trying to get ready for the show."

"Sorry, Roxy," Mitchell said, his smile tensing. "But you might not be having a show at all if not for this fortunate twist, so just deal with it."

"It's fine," Sadie said, hoping to deescalate the disagreement. "I understand, and I'll explain it to Coco."

Somehow Mitchell managed to frown in confusion while maintaining a smile that looked less genuine by the second. "OK. But do me a favor and come out to the lobby during the second act, so I can go over this at the table. Not at intermission. There'll be people out there having refreshments. Wait until the second act starts." He turned to walk away, his smile gone before he'd even made a full about face.

Alex hurried toward his dressing room. At the sight of Roxy, he slowed down and attempted to pass quietly behind her.

"You're late, Alex," Roxy said without so much as turning her head.

"I'm here now," Alex retorted. "That's more than you can say about Nevada. She's out in the alley arguing with that detective."

"This is how the two of you act when you get to take over the leads?" Roxy shook her head, exasperated.

"We didn't have a choice, and like I said, I'm here now." Alex slung a jacket over his shoulder and disappeared down the hall.

"Wow," Sadie sighed. "Is everyone anxious because of Detective Higgins?"

Roxy pulled her headset down behind her neck and let it rest above her shoulders. She stretched her head from side to side. "No, though that's a big part of it. It's unnerving having police hanging around. But the show's success is up in the air. If tonight doesn't go over, the rest of the play's run could be cancelled."

"Oh, my," Sadie said. "I didn't think of that."

"There's always a possibility. Ernie could pull the plug." Roxy shot off a quick cue reminder to the sound techs.

"But he must want the show to go on," Sadie said. "He's thrilled that Nevada has the lead now, right?"

"Sure, Ernie's thrilled Nevada took over Brynn's part." Roxy said. "But not thrilled enough to lose money. As I said before, the almighty dollar is always Ernie's bottom line." Roxy reached around her neck and pulled the headset back onto her head, positioning the microphone in front of her mouth. "Thirty minutes to curtain."

"I'd better check on Coco." Sadie looked around at the increased pace backstage.

"I'm sure she's still sitting right where she was, admiring herself in the mirror," Roxy said. "You've got quite a character on your hands."

"No argument there," Sadie said.

Much to Sadie's relief, Coco was, indeed, right where she'd left her, in front of the dressing room mirror. Although she was standing now, it was clear she'd been lying down, as the bow on her head was slightly askew.

"Let's straighten this before Freda sees you." Sadie removed the pins holding the bow and, trying it on herself before returning it to Coco, she secured it back on the Yorkie's head. "There, much better. No napping now." Coco licked Sadie's hand, and Sadie rewarded her with a treat.

Coop entered, picnic basket in one hand. He set the basket on the floor and opened the lid. Coco jumped down from the dressing table and right into the wicker container.

"You see?" Sadie beamed. "She knows her part."

"Sid asked to have her practice again, and I want to test the speaker one more time." Coop shuffled a few items around Coco and closed the lid. Coop adjusted Sadie's headset and took a position on the floor similar to those in the picnic scene. "Go ahead and give her the command."

"Give toys," Sadie said into her headset.

Coco stuck her head out of the basket and ducked back inside.

Coop and Roxy exchanged panicked looks. Both breathed sighs of relief when Coco popped back up, this time hopping out and presenting Coop with a plastic spoon.

"Good girl," Sadie said. Proud of her trick, the Yorkie returned to the basket and jumped back inside.

"Try it from outside the door," Coop said, "so I can make sure she's responding to your voice speaker, not you directly."

Sadie stepped into the hall, gave the command, and came back into the room. She found Coop holding a paper napkin. Coco sat in the picnic basket, an object in her mouth. Sadie did a double take.

"Is that a comb in her mouth?"

Coop nodded. "Apparently she's expanding on the game. She delivered the napkin, but then pulled a comb out of my pocket and took it back with her."

"Oh, dear," Sadie said. "Yes, she does like to find items to store in her basket at home sometimes. I never know what I'll find in there, aside from her favorite stuffed lobster toy." She looked at Coco, and then back at Coop, worried. "Is this going to be a problem?"

"I don't think so." Coop stood up. "Just something else to amuse the audience."

A knock on the door interrupted the conversation.

"Ten minutes to curtain."

"Thanks. Ten," Coop replied. He turned to Sadie. "Keep Coco with you here. I'll come get her one scene before the picnic." Sadie lifted Coco out of the basket as Coop picked it up. "I need to set this on the prop table for now." He paused, looking inside. "I'll take this back." He lifted the comb out, slipped it into his pocket and looked in the basket again. "And...I believe this goes here..." He pulled a makeup brush out and placed it on the dressing table.

"Anything else interesting in there?" Sadie said.

Coop rummaged through the remaining items. "Nope, nothing but picnic supplies now." He disappeared into the hallway, closing the dressing room door behind him.

"You're such a clever girl," Sadie said, patting Coco on the head, though careful not to disturb the sequined bow. She set Coco down on the floor and turned to a compact refrigerator and small microwave in the corner of the room. She pulled a serving of chocolate lava cake from the refrigerator and removed the plastic wrap. She had warned the crew to keep chocolate away from Coco, as it wasn't good for dogs, and had been pleased to see the desserts stashed safely away. Popping the cake into the microwave, she heated it twenty seconds, just enough to give the "lava" description meaning. Sitting down at the dressing table, she took a bite and settled in to wait for further instructions.

"Everything good?" Roxy said, sticking her head in quickly.

"Fine, we're ready," Sadie replied. Coco yipped, as well.

Sadie watched Roxy disappear as rapidly as she'd appeared. Returning to the cake, she scooped another bite into her mouth, closing her eyes to savor the rich flavor. Again she took a generous bite, repeating her closed-eye appreciation. One bite at a time, she finished off the decadent dessert. *There's nothing in the world better than chocolate*, she mused. Sighing, she opened her eyes and looked around.

"Coco?" Sadie scanned the room. "Where are you hiding?" She set the empty cake plate on top of the microwave and looked under the dressing table. No sign of the petite dog under that piece of furniture or any other. The wastebasket was empty, as well. It was worth looking there; it was a basket, after all. Sadie studied the room, finally noticing the door to the hallway was ajar. Panic kicked in as she realized Roxy, in her haste, had not closed the door all the way.

Sadie stuck her head out into the hallway. "Coco?" she whispered. The first scene already under way, she could hear the actors delivering their lines from the stage. Shouting Coco's name was out of the question.

"Have you seen a small dog?" she whispered to a crew member passing by. The young man's eyes widened as he shook his head and hurried on.

Sadie reached the area just behind the stage and tiptoed in. She dropped to her hands and knees and began checking under chairs and inside containers. A tall stack of coiled electrical cords looked promising, but close inspection revealed nothing inside. She continued to crawl along the wall, peeking sideways at the hanging curtains leading to the stage. She could see glimpses of the actors and hear their voices echoing. She flattened her head against the floor as she came up alongside each curtain, checking to see if Coco might be hovering between the fabric and the floor. The rascal was small enough to hide there. Why hadn't she adopted a Great Dane instead of a Yorkie? There'd be no chance of losing that critter backstage.

"What on *earth* are you doing?"

Sadie's clear vision of the stage suddenly became a dark silhouette of a shoe. She gulped and stood up, dismayed to find herself face to face with Sid. "I…I lost something," she said. No other explanation came to mind and, besides, it was true. She *had* lost something.

"Maybe you could wait to find it later?" Sid practically hissed. "We have a show in progress now, in case you didn't notice."

Coop came to the rescue. "Don't worry, Sid, I found the item she lost." He took Sadie's elbow as Sid threw his hands up in the air and stalked off.

"This way," Coop whispered, pulling Sadie back to the prop table. There, sitting calmly in the picnic basket, was an innocent-looking Coco.

"Roxy poked her head into the dressing room to check on us," Sadie sputtered, trying to apologize. "She must have left the door open."

"No harm done," Coop said. "At least she's ready for her entrance. But do stay right here with her, OK? Sid will have my job if it happens again. Or if he finds out about this time, for that matter."

"Absolutely," Sadie promised. Coop walked away, leaving Sadie looking down at the wayward canine. As Coco tilted her head upwards and gazed lovingly at her human, Sadie could swear she saw a smile emerge amidst the fur.

CHAPTER THIRTEEN

Sadie stood by the prop table, one hand resting carefully on Coco's head, just behind the sequined bow. Bumping the headpiece off kilter at this point was bound to upset Freda, and possibly other company members who were skeptical about Coco's involvement. Penelope, for example, had given Coco a look that was anything but warm earlier, when they'd first walked by the box office. Sadie still couldn't figure out what the girl's problem was, still suspecting she was a wannabe star.

A voice as clear as a wind chime and sweet as a morning sparrow came floating from the stage. Ah, Sadie thought. Nevada had just launched into song, which meant the show was midway through the second scene. Her singing voice was ten times better than Brynn's. Again, it was obvious Sid should have cast her for the lead instead of Brynn. How many people resented his decision?

Sadie mulled this over as she waited for the show's first act to progress. Alex had joined in song with Nevada, and Sadie paid more attention to his voice this night than she had before. As was the case with Nevada, his delivery was clearer and stronger than Russell's had been. It seemed favoritism weighed more than talent when Sid cast both leads. It dawned on Sadie for the first time that Alex may have resented Sid's casting choices, as well. Ernie hadn't mentioned Alex at all in the conversation she'd overheard at Curtain Call the day she arrived for the dress rehearsal. Perhaps he wasn't concerned about the leading man role. Maybe he didn't understand how casting the male lead would have affected Nevada if Sid *had* put her in Brynn's role.

"Warning picnic scene." Roxy's voice interrupted her thoughts. A minute later Coop reappeared at the table to fetch the picnic basket. Sadie's nerves kicked in, and she had trouble releasing the basket.

"It'll be fine," Coop assured her. "Remember, I'm in this scene. I'll take Coco out when we set the stage. And I'll be sitting nearby. In fact, I'll be closest to the picnic basket."

"How do we know she won't pop out early?" Sadie asked. "We should have practiced telling her to 'stay' until it was time for her to pop out." A dozen scenarios of things going wrong flew through Sadie's mind within seconds.

"I'll take care of that," Coop said.

This comforted Sadie, at least as much as it was possible to be comforted, knowing she was letting Coco out into a murder scene. She shivered at this thought as she watched Coop head into the wings. Maybe agreeing to Sid and Mitchell's scheme wasn't such a great idea. Yet she'd signed a contract. She'd let her excitement at the idea of Coco's stardom interfere with rational thought. There was nothing she could do about it now, except hope everything would be OK.

Sadie took a deep breath and moved into the wings, positioning herself near Roxy, who signaled for her to stay quiet.

"Standby." Roxy's voice was calm and focused. Sadie watched as the stage lights faded to black. Several figures carried props onto the stage, including Coop, who set the picnic basket down and sat on the floor beside it.

"Go picnic scene," Roxy said.

The stage lights came up, revealing the scene Sadie had watched twice before: at the dress rehearsal, uneventful except for the spilled lemonade, and the night before, most definitely eventful with Coco's surprise performance. The setting was a lively one, with the full cast spread around the stage. Several actors sat at a picnic table in animated conversation with each other. Two others nearby tossed a beach ball back and forth. Nevada, Alex, Coop, and a few others sat on a blanket on the floor. Nevada turned the pages of a book while Alex stretched out, enjoying the imaginary sun. Coop leaned casually over the picnic basket, one elbow on the lid, fist under his chin as he conversed with the closest person at the table.

"Stay," Sadie whispered into her headset, just for good measure, though Coop's clever pose would prevent Coco from entering early.

"Standby light cue 18A" Roxy shifted her stance as the lighting booth confirmed the standby call.

"Go lights." Roxy smiled at Sadie as a spotlight brightened over the picnic basket. Coop straightened up, stretching both arms over his head. The lid on the basket flapped up and down slightly. Sadie tensed, wondering if the lid felt heavier to Coco this time. If she couldn't get out, they were all in trouble.

"Let's see what we have for lunch," Coop said, picking up on the potential problem. "I'm famished." Other picnic-goers chimed in. Coop lifted the picnic basket lid and Coco's bow popped up, seemingly unattached to a head, and then disappeared back into the basket. A second later, however, both her bow and head appeared, much to the delight of the audience.

"Oh!" Nevada squealed with delight. "Fluffy, there you are!"

Fluffy again? Sadie thought. *Really?* Why hadn't she thought to specify a different name in Coco's contract? Maybe it really was time to get Coco an agent. These things could be negotiated.

Sadie felt Roxy elbow her. Though not as official as the light and sound cues Roxy had been calling, the meaning was clear.

"Give toys," Sadie said into her headset.

Coco dropped back inside the basket. Roxy sucked in her breath as they all waited for Coco to do her part. Sadie bit her lip and tapped one hand nervously against her side. But a few seconds later, Coco appeared with the grapes from the night before. Propping her two front paws on the basket's rim, she scrambled over the edge and landed on the stage with the finesse of an Olympic gymnast. Applause filled the theatre as Coco delivered the grapes to Nevada, then trotted back to the basket and hopped in.

"Give toys," Sadie said again. Dutifully, Coco jumped out, this time with a green leaf in her mouth, the stem attached to an object that remained stubbornly inside the basket. Not to be dissuaded, Coco gripped the leaf with her teeth and pulled, but nothing happened. She tried again. Still nothing. She let go of the leaf and faced the audience as a round of "aws" circled the theatre. Then, like a fox jumping for prey, she turned back, grabbed the leaf and tugged with her full body weight, slight as it was. She fell back onto the floor with the leaf still firmly gripped between her teeth. An orange popped over the side of the basket and rolled forward, pulling Coco into a somersault.

The audience roared. It was all the encouragement she needed. One by one, she pulled surprises from the basket, distributing them around the stage. She delivered paper napkins to those at the picnic table, which they passed around to each other. Alex received a plastic cup, into which another cast member poured lemonade, this time without spilling it. And Coop seemed delighted when Coco surprised him with a tape measure.

"I wondered where that went," Freda said, standing behind Sadie and Roxy.

As a finale, Coco pulled a sandwich from the basket, carrying it around the stage in its clear baggie. Going from one cast member to the next, she appeared to contemplate who should receive this special gift. Finally, she walked toward the edge of the stage and sat down, shaking the plastic bag from side to side until it ripped open.

"Oh, no," a young male crew member to Sadie's left said. "I…"

"Shhh!" Roxy cautioned just before the sandwich went flying across the floor. Coco immediately chased after it, bringing it back to center stage, where she placed one paw on its edge and took a bite. Looking up, she smacked her lips and went back for more.

"I'm confused," Roxy said. "Isn't that plastic? We use a plastic sandwich for that prop. I hope she doesn't get sick."

"You and me both," Sadie said.

"At least not on stage," Sid mumbled, also watching nearby.

"That's what I was trying to say," the same young man said. "I couldn't find the one we usually use, so I just threw my own sandwich in as a substitute."

"What kind?" Sadie asked.

"Peanut butter." The young man looked at Sadie apologetically.

Sadie smiled. "Her favorite."

To thunderous applause, the curtain came down for intermission. Sadie rushed out onto the stage and snatched up the canine star. Coco clung stubbornly to the remaining half sandwich with her teeth, but looked up at Sadie with both pride in her eyes and peanut butter on her mouth.

"Good job, Coco," Sadie said. "Now let's get you cleaned up."

* * *

The Pawtograph table turned out to be just as successful as everyone hoped. Mitchell stood by grinning proudly, as if he were the one dipping a paw into ink and pressing it firmly inside each person's program. Coco lapped up the attention, kissing anyone who would let her and even those who didn't want doggie kisses.

Roxy approached as the crowd was thinning out. Sid and Ernie had both stopped by to congratulate Coco on the performance, patting her on the head and thanking Sadie as an afterthought. Freda came out to retrieve the rhinestone collar and sequined bows, but Mitchell shooed her away, citing Coco's costume needs for photo ops.

"Everyone's meeting at Curtain Call," Roxy said. "Coco's invited. And you. In that order." Roxy laughed as Sadie rolled her eyes.

"Dogs aren't allowed in food establishments, you know," Sadie said. "I don't want to get you guys in trouble." She lifted Coco's non-inked paw up so that a guest could shake it.

"Don't worry. Ernie's arranged a private party," Roxy said. "The café's making an exception, since they won't be open to the public. They also want a pawtographed headshot to add to the collection on their wall."

"Coco doesn't have a headshot," Sadie pointed out.

"We can use one of the show flyers," Roxy said. "They'll have a headshot done up for her by next week."

Sadie blinked. "Wait. Did you just say 'next week'?"

"Oh, right." Roxy squeezed Sadie's shoulder. "Sid's going to talk to you about that." Roxy scooted off before Sadie could ask for clarification.

CHAPTER FOURTEEN

A noisy crowd of cast and crew filled Curtain Call. Champagne splashed from flutes as the rambunctious group shared tidbits from the weekend's events. Brynn's murder, the show's opening, Russell's arrest, and Coco's newfound fame, meant there was no shortage of conversation topics. On the café's counter were platters of cheese, crackers and fruit. Bowls of chips and dips were spread around the room on individual tables.

"This must be the cast party that Sid mentioned," Sadie said to Roxy as they walked in.

"No, that's not until next weekend. After the next two shows."

"The next what?"

"That's what Sid's planning to discuss with you." Roxy patted Sadie on the back. "In fact, here he comes now."

Sadie saw Sid emerging from the crowd like a shark from a wave. Instinctively, she looked around for a place to hide.

"Sadie, so great to see you!" Sadie snagged a champagne flute from the nearest beverage cart and let Sid drag her through the crowd to a table in the back. She wasn't surprised to find Ernie and Mitchell both seated already. Two chairs had been saved – one for Sadie, and one for Coco.

"Great job, you two," Mitchell said, his gaze falling on Sadie, as well as the tote bag she'd just placed on the other empty chair.

"You're talking to a purse, Mitch." Sid smirked as he tipped back his glass, which was heavier than the champagne flutes making the rounds. Ernie and Mitchell had similar barware. Sid pulled a flask from his jacket pocket and splashed a refill into each tumbler.

"And a fine purse it is, too," Ernie said. "Let's see that little star you have in there." As always, Sadie could almost see dollar signs replacing his pupils.

Sadie lifted an exhausted looking Coco out of the tote and set the Yorkie in her lap. Coco looked around and then leaned against Sadie, closing her eyes. "She's had a big night, guys. I'm not sure she'll last long here." Sadie stroked Coco's head, now devoid of sequins, which Freda had confiscated the moment the last pawtograph was given out.

"We understand," Mitchell said. "And we want her to get her beauty sleep. Isn't that right?" He looked at Sid and Ernie.

"Absolutely," Sid said.

Ernie nodded in and then spoke. "Ms...."

"Just Sadie is fine." How many times would she need to tell the producer her name?

"Sadie," Ernie continued. "I'm sure you'll be pleased to hear we're going to pick up the option on Coco's contract."

Sadie ran through her mind the details her lawyer had explained when she first emailed him a copy of the contract. Was that really only the previous morning? It felt like a week had passed since they'd arrived.

"Yes, I remember what the option means. You're allowed to extend Coco's role in the show." Sadie's thoughts drifted to Flair and to San Francisco. She couldn't possibly stay in Monterey a full week. Why hadn't she thought this through before?

"Exactly," Ernie said. "That's how it works. The show tonight was a smashing success, just as it was last night. I saw people buying tickets on the way out, so they could bring friends back with them next weekend."

Sadie inspected Coco's ink-stained paw, thinking through the logistics. "I have a business to run in San Francisco."

"You don't need to stay here for the week," Sid explained. "There won't be any additional rehearsals. Coco seems quite capable of doing her own thing. You just need to be back here Friday afternoon. Same schedule as tonight. Six o'clock call time."

Sadie mulled this over. It would work, not that she had a choice. She'd run Flair during the week and return to Monterey the following weekend. Besides, it would give her a chance to poke around and see what she could find out about Brynn's murder. She scanned the crowd, curious to see if Detective Higgins was hanging around. She saw no sign of him.

"Just two shows, correct?" Sadie asked, focusing on the discussion again. Coco curled up in her lap and closed her eyes.

"Yes," Ernie said. "That's the end of the run. Unfortunately," he added. "I'm sure we could sell out another ten shows."

"At least," Mitchell added.

"Fine," Sadie said. "We'll be here. Maybe you could give Alex some kind of allergy pill to keep him from sneezing."

"Oh, that won't be necessary," Ernie said. "Russell will be playing the part next week. Alex goes back to understudy and his regular role. Our boy just needed tonight off. He's been distraught, as you can imagine. Hauled off to jail, and all that."

"He was quite fond of Brynn, too, wasn't he?" Mitchell added.

"Indeed," Ernie said.

Sid looked down at a flashy ring on his right hand and spun it around his finger with his thumb. Sadie wondered what the mention of Brynn and Russell in the same sentence meant to Sid. Grief? Jealousy?

"Yes, I believe he was," Sid said, his face expressionless. He pulled the flask from his jacket again and refilled his own drink but didn't offer more to the others.

"I 'gree." Nevada's voice took Sadie by surprise. It was the same sweet voice she used on stage, only a few champagne glasses down the line. "He was cr..azzzy about her," Nevada slurred. She leaned over Coco to give her a kiss, hitting her head on the edge of the table in the process. "Ow." She straightened up, rubbing her forehead.

"Nevada." Ernie frowned. "I think it's time to switch to coffee."

"Oh, I will, Unc' Ernie," Nevada said. "After justa fewww more." She lifted her glass in a salute and turned away, stumbling over to a table where Alex sat. She attempted to kiss Alex as she dropped into a chair, but Alex turned his head away.

Interesting, Sadie thought.

"I'm sorry about that," Ernie said. "She gets out of hand sometimes."

"Relax," Sid said. "It's a party, and she's an adult. And a pretty one at that."

"Just like you to defend drinking," Ernie snapped. "And you keep your hands off her."

'Well, I don't see soda water in that glass of yours," Sid retorted. "And Nevada's a big girl. I'll keep my hands off her if she tells me to. It's not like you own either of us."

Sadie decided to move on, before the conversation deteriorated further. "We'd better make the rounds," she said, standing up. "Coco has fans, you know." She lifted the tote bag off the chair, keeping Coco curled up against her chest. Assuring Sid, Mitchell and Ernie that she'd see them on Friday, she crossed the room. Pausing to let Coco accept a few congratulatory pats on the head, she finally slid into a table with Roxy and Coop.

"I saw that little confrontation," Roxy said. "It's kind of strange, Nevada getting drunk like that. I haven't seen her overindulge before. Usually, it's one glass of something alcoholic, and then she moves on to tonic with lime. I wonder what's up."

"She's upset," Coop said.

"Upset? Why?" Sadie looked at Coop, confused. "She seemed fine on stage. Did something happen after the show?"

"Not after, before," Coop said. "She's a good actress; that's why it wasn't obvious during the show. But she and Higgins got into it earlier."

Sadie nodded. "That's right. I remember Alex made a comment about seeing her in the alley, arguing with Detective Higgins." She turned to Roxy. "You remember that?"

"Let's see," Roxy quipped. "You mean when he tried to sneak in late?"

"Yes, exactly," Sadie said. "And, come to think of it, he didn't sound all too happy about Nevada being out there."

Roxy laughed. "That's because he knew she wouldn't get in trouble. Sid never comes down on her for anything. She gets away with whatever she wants. If Alex were a pretty girl, he would, too. But he can't pull that with me. And he's lucky Sid didn't see him."

"Are you sure that's all it was?" Sadie paused, thinking back to Alex's expression when he walked by, the way he moved, the way he slung his jacket over his shoulder. He looked annoyed, perhaps even angry. Or was it worry she'd seen on his face?

"I don't see what else it could be," Roxy said. "He just didn't like getting caught missing the call time."

"Maybe he overheard something on his way in that upset him," Sadie suggested. "Something in the conversation between Nevada and Detective Higgins." *Something incriminating*, Sadie thought.

"Well, speak of the devil," Coop said, nodding toward the front door.

Sadie and Roxy both turned to see Higgins enter. Although a few people looked up when he came in, most of the company went right back to their champagne and conversation. Higgins turned down a drink, but helped himself to cheese and crackers. He leaned against the front counter, his eyes casually scanning the crowd.

"I don't see what he thinks he can find out tonight," Roxy said. "He's already grilled everyone in the show."

"He didn't stop by for nothing," Coop said. "He must think he'll learn something from someone here."

"Maybe," Sadie said. "Or, more likely, from someone not here." She looked at the table where Nevada and Alex had just been sitting. The seats were empty, and the back door to the café was ajar.

CHAPTER FIFTEEN

Sadie adjusted the rear view mirror and looked at the road ahead. She loved driving Highway One, whether she was heading north from San Francisco, or south. This time, northbound from Monterey, she stepped on the gas, anxious to get home to the city. Despite the luxurious hotel, she was ready to be in familiar territory, and to rest. She had plenty to do at the boutique. And plenty to think about.

It hadn't taken her long to pack up that morning. The night before at Curtain Call, after she'd noticed that Nevada and Alex had slipped away, Sadie had only stayed fifteen more minutes. She used Coco's need for beauty sleep as an excuse.

She'd reserved three nights at the hotel for the following weekend: Friday and Saturday for the shows, and Thursday to accommodate some extra time to snoop. She had several different theories about the events behind Brynn Baker's sudden demise, none including the word "accident." Now, she just needed to sort fiction from fact. This wasn't an easy task under usual circumstances, but with a cast of characters trained to present false fronts, the challenge reached new levels. At least in most cases – dare she say "cases" when she just happened to fall into these situations? – she only had to decipher motives, without incorporating professional acting into the equation. The addition of suspects who were proficient at make believe meant that she needed to do some real investigating rather than relying solely on what she saw and heard in person.

Sadie went directly to Flair instead of stopping first at her penthouse apartment. Sundays were the only days the boutique didn't open. As much as she adored Amber and her regular customers, the closed sign on the door was a relief. She welcomed time alone in the shop on this particular day. She could zip into the back office to check a few things without feeling the urge to chitchat with anyone.

She unbuckled the harness she used to keep her tote secure and lifted the bag off the car's passenger seat. When she peeked inside, she wasn't surprised to see Coco fast asleep. It had been a hectic weekend, and the petite canine was prone to getting sleepy on road trips, anyway. Stepping lightly, to avoid waking Coco, she used her shop key to enter, then locked the door behind her and scooted back to her office.

Three notes waited on her desk: one from Amber, welcoming her back, another from a customer who wanted to special order a certain style sweater in a color Sadie knew would not be available, and a third from Matteo, her friend and next door chocolatier. It seemed during her absence, he'd been developing a new truffle, one with mango, coconut and pecans that she simply had to try. Relieved to see Matteo had left samples with the note, she popped one in her mouth and sighed with appreciation. When it came to chocolate, Matteo knew what he was doing. Still, she wasn't sorry she'd ordered two servings of chocolate lava cake to go before leaving the hotel. Those would be perfect for late-night snacking during the week.

Sadie flipped through her address book, contemplating a call to one of several private detectives she'd used over the years to gather information when she stumbled into mysteries. Vetoing the idea, she put the book away and fired up the office computer. After multiple internet searches, she'd gathered background information on everyone in the cast. Almost, that is. Oddly enough, she couldn't find anything on Nevada, at least not under the name Nevada Foster. She tried variations – N. Foster, Neve Foster, etc.

Nothing. Fiddling with the chunky beaded earrings she'd donned early that morning, she pondered the meaning of this. Was the girl using a stage name? A false name? Was she concealing her true identity for some reason, and, if so, what was that reason?

Shutting down the computer, she pocketed a second mango-coconut-pecan truffle and grabbed her tote bag. Coco had begun snoring like a miniature freight train and was ready for her own dog bed. Sadie didn't mind the idea of her own bed, either. She locked up the shop and headed home.

As much as she loved excursions, she was always pleased to come home. The penthouse apartment she lived in was luxurious and spacious, with breathtaking views. Marrying an investment banker many years ago had left her in a secure financial position once she became a widow. She looked out over the bay and sighed. She still missed him, even though her escapades kept her busy and Coco kept her company.

Sadie unpacked her overnight bag, which took only a few minutes, since she'd not anticipated staying in Monterey more than one night. It took a little more time to put away the five large bags of new purchases from the shopping expedition she'd made when she learned her stay would be extended. Setting aside the two black outfits she'd worn backstage, which would need to be laundered, she pulled out a variety of items she hadn't been able to resist. It felt like Christmas, seeing one item after the next – flat shoes in a fiery red with silver buckles, a stunning leather purse with gold studded trim, a dangling necklace with a giant green frog, along with earrings shaped like lily pads. She was always surprised at how delightful it was to dive into bags of her purchases when she got home, as if she were discovering all the fabulous items for the first time.

Once she stored her new acquisitions in her closet, Sadie changed into a favorite lounging outfit, a flowing hot pink robe with boa trim. She returned to the living room, where she found Coco tossing her stuffed red lobster in the air by gripping one claw between her teeth. Each time the plush toy flew through the air Coco chased after it, brought it back to the starting point, and began the game all over again.

With Coco occupied, Sadie poured herself a glass of chardonnay from a bottle she'd saved after a recent trip to Napa Valley. It had been hours since she'd left Monterey, hours during which new developments in the Brynn Baker investigation could have arisen. Sadie decided to call Roxy. Roxy answered on the second ring.

"Anything new since I left?" Sadie asked. She leaned back in an armchair and sipped her wine while she waited for Roxy to respond.

"It's Sunday, Sadie," Roxy said. "Not a lot happens on Sunday. And you only left this morning."

"I realize that, but you never know. Something could have come up, some tidbit of information." She took another sip of wine and set the glass down on an end table.

"Well, now that you mention it, there is one thing." Roxy lowered her voice, which struck Sadie as odd, since she assumed Roxy had answered her phone at home.

"Where are you that you have to whisper?" Sadie asked.

"At Curtain Call," Roxy said. "I came down to get soup and a sandwich to go. I plan to do nothing tonight except eat dinner in pajamas and watch movies. I'm debating between *The Sound of Music* and *Funny Girl.*"

"Sounds like a perfect evening to me," Sadie admitted. All things considered, she might do exactly the same thing. Except she'd order in pizza, and she and Coco would watch *Lady and the Tramp* or *Beethoven.* "So what was the one thing you were about to tell me?"

"Oh, just a minute," Roxy said. The sound of a cash register ringing followed, as well as Roxy saying "thank you" and exiting the café. Sadie heard the rumpling sound of a paper bag. "I checked the cleaning schedule for the day of the dress rehearsal, and the cleaning service was booked for that day."

"Which means – if the schedule was followed – that Penelope did not clean the theatre that night," Sadie said. "So she wouldn't have had a reason to be backstage."

"That's the way I see it," Roxy said.

"So it's unlikely she was anywhere near the catwalk," Sadie said, "or even swiped Russell's phone. That is, if anyone *did* swipe it, as he claims."

"Right, and he still insists someone did," Roxy said.

"Did the police or Russell ever say what was on Brynn's phone that made him a suspect?" Sadie asked.

"Higgins never specified. Said it was part of the ongoing investigation," Roxy said. "And Russell won't say. He says it's not important, especially since he claims he wasn't the one who sent the text."

"Sounds like Russell doesn't want to say what it was," Sadie mused. "Maybe he feels it's something incriminating. But why would it matter, if he doesn't have anything to hide?"

Roxy sighed. "Well, something can make someone look guilty, even if he's innocent."

"True," Sadie said. "And someone can insist he's being wrongly accused, even if he's guilty."

"Exactly."

"What do *you* think, Roxy? You know everyone in the cast much better than I do." Sadie reached for her wine glass as she watched Coco set her stuffed lobster aside and return to her dog bed for a nap.

"Honestly, Sadie, I don't know what to think. Now I do think Russell was the one seeing Brynn secretly, and not Alex. If so, it doesn't make sense that he'd want her dead. And Sid was angry when she dumped him, but I don't think he would kill off one of the show's main stars."

"What about Ernie Palmer," Sadie asked. "He wanted Nevada to have the lead. Getting Brynn out of the way would be a quick means to that end."

"I can't see Ernie risking it. The night before a show opens is a tough time to lose a cast member," Roxy said. "No matter how prepared an understudy is. Ernie's always so concerned about finances."

"And Nevada?" Sadie asked.

"What about Nevada?" Roxy said. "You don't think...No, that is too far-fetched. I know she was disappointed when she didn't get the lead, but resorting to murder? No, I don't see it."

"I know you like the girl, Roxy, but I found something curious this afternoon."

After a pause, Roxy said, "Curious in what way?"

"I did background checks on all the main cast members. But I couldn't find anything online about Nevada. It's like she never existed."

"How odd," Roxy said. "She has a decent-looking resume. Not a lot of experience, but she's young, and she's had a few decent parts."

"Do directors check resumes before they cast people?" Sadie asked. "Like references for a regular job?"

"Usually, I think," Roxy said. "I never thought about it. I only handle the backstage stuff. I hire people the regular way. Since Ernie pretty much sponsored her, maybe no one bothered checking."

"Ernie probably made it clear he'd only back the show with her in it," Sadie pointed out. "Maybe they didn't check her references or previous jobs on her resume because it didn't matter. If they hadn't cast Nevada, whoever she is, Sid and Mitchell wouldn't have gotten Ernie's financial backing. If this is true, Sid and Mitchell would have figured they didn't have a choice."

"You may be on to something there," Roxy said. "I never thought about it."

"On the other hand..." Sadie said, thinking this over. "Coco would disagree."

"OK." Roxy's tone was skeptical. "Why do you say that?"

"Because Coco took to Nevada right away on stage, during that first...uh...mishap. Dogs have a keen sense about people."

"Right...the *mishap*." Roxy laughed. "Well, you and Coco keep me posted on your theories, all right?"

"You've got it," Sadie quipped. "We'll continue our investigation and let you know if we make any progress."

"Great, you do that," Roxy said. "I'm off to investigate how long it takes the microwave to warm up the soup that got cold while we've been talking."

The call over, Sadie stood and stretched, the boa neck trim tickling her face as she raised her arms over her head. She relaxed and looked at Coco, who slept with the finesse of a trapeze artist, upper body and front legs flopped in one direction, lower body and hind legs twisted in the other.

"You do have a good sense about people, right?" Sadie whispered to the canine contortionist. "I'm counting on you for this one, Coco. It's awfully strange that Nevada Foster – or whatever her name is – seems to have appeared out of nowhere, financial backing or not."

A light snore was the only response Sadie received. For now, it would have to be enough.

CHAPTER SIXTEEN

"Fill me in," Amber said as Sadie walked in the door to Flair. "What have you gotten yourself wrapped up in this time?" Her arm swirled in energetic circles as she cleaned the store's glass display counter. A spray bottle of blue liquid stood nearby.

"Good morning to you, too," Sadie laughed, familiar with her assistant's morning fervor. "How many cups today?"

"Only three," Amber said before looking up and smiling. "OK, maybe five. But only one with a double shot. You know I can't resist the coffee at Jay's Java Joint. And, yes, before you ask, I only made decaf in the back."

"Good news for sure," Sadie said. "I think I'll grab a cup." She paused to deliver Coco to the velvet pillow on the front counter. With all the attention she received from customers, it wasn't a stretch to figure out why it was the Yorkie's favorite daytime location.

"Cute shoes!" Amber called out as Sadie stepped into the back office and poured a mug of decaf.

"Thank you. I dare say I agree," Sadie said as she emerged from the back. "Cutest little store in Carmel. It's pet-friendly, too, which Coco loved. They carry a great line of jewelry that I didn't have time to peruse. I must go back this weekend. Speaking of which…"

Amber laughed. "Let me guess. Your new star has a repeat performance lined up." She gave Coco a pat on the head. Sadie could swear she saw Coco lift her chin upwards in a display of pride.

"Two, actually." Sadie lifted one hand to indicate "two" with her fingers. Gold bangles clattered against each other as she did. She'd added them just before she left the penthouse to brighten what was for her an uncharacteristically plain outfit: blue jeans and a solid black sweater. "I wish you could make it to one of the shows. Coco has such a fabulous stage presence!"

"I'm sure she does."

"Meanwhile, what's new here? Anything going on?" Sadie was pleased with the shop's appearance. She could always count on Amber to keep it neat and tidy.

"Nothing unusual," Amber said. "We have some UPS deliveries coming in this afternoon. The earrings from Ecuador, for one."

"Ooh, the ones with the exotic birds?"

"Yep. And a fill-in order of cardigans — several sizes and colors that were sold out. Oh, Mrs. Jennings left you a note about getting one in lavender."

Sadie nodded. "Yes, I saw that yesterday when I popped in. She'll have to settle for deep purple or just pick another color."

"Matteo left you samples of a new truffle."

"Yes, delicious!" Sadie exclaimed. "Thank goodness he left four of them. I took some home with me."

"Well, actually, he left six…" Amber grinned.

"All the more reason for me to go next door and pick up some more! The sooner the better, I think." Sadie popped back into the office and pulled several bills from her wallet. Passing Amber on the way out, she promised to bring back an assortment to share with customers during the day.

* * *

Matteo Tremiato looked up from behind the counter at Cioccolato and grinned when Sadie entered. "I knew it wouldn't take you long to come over. You like the new truffle?"

"Have you ever made a truffle I didn't like?" Sadie walked straight to the display case and looked over the selection. It varied from day to day, depending on what new treats Matteo concocted. Today's options met her approval: Raspberry Cream, Cocoa Mint, Peanut Butter Crunch, Lemon Tart, and his new masterpiece, Mango-Pineapple-Pecan. "I'll take two of each, but give me four of that new one."

"One dozen truffles coming up," Matteo said. He pulled a gift box from under the counter, inserted a waxed paper liner, and filled it with the requested assortment. "Half price, as always," he said.

Sadie smiled. This was a perfectly acceptable arrangement, as far as she was concerned. She received chocolate at a discount, and her boutique customers took Matteo's business card when they tried samples. She had an endless chocolate supply, her customers were thrilled, and Matteo gained new fans. It was a win-win-win.

"How's the little celebrity doing?" Matteo asked as he rang up the order and handed Sadie her box of chocolates.

"Ah, you know already." Sadie grinned.

Matteo nodded. "Amber told me, plus I read about it in the morning paper."

"Oh!" Sadie squealed. "How exciting! Front page?"

"No," Matteo said, holding back a laugh. "A small blurb, several pages in. And it was mostly about that awful murder. But there was a brief mention of a dog adding some levity to the otherwise tragic situation."

"Yes, that was Coco's stage debut," Sadie said.

"I take it this wasn't planned." Matteo smiled as he handed Sadie her change.

"No," Sadie said. "Coco just happened to escape the dressing room where she was supposed to wait for me, and she got loose on stage. Actually, she stowed away in a picnic basket that was a prop for one scene."

"And now she's part of the show?"

"Yes!" Sadie exclaimed. "Isn't that fabulous? She has two more shows this coming weekend, Friday and Saturday. So we'll go back down to Monterey on Thursday."

"Let me guess," Matteo said. "A day early, so that you can poke around for information about that murder?"

"How did you know, Matteo?" Sadie laughed. Her reputation for sleuthing was well established. Matteo was especially aware of this, since Sadie had recently helped solve a crime at his family's winery.

Returning to Flair, Sadie gave Amber the box of truffles to offer customers at the front counter, patted Coco on the head, and went back to her office. She sat at her desk and booted up the computer. A thought about Nevada Foster's information – or lack of information, more precisely – kept nagging her. It just didn't make sense that she hadn't been able to dig up any background on the girl the night before.

Nevada Foster
N. Foster
Neva Foster
Neva da Foster

No matter how she spelled the actress' name, nothing came up. She drummed her fingers on the desk from her pinky to index finger. This galloping sound used to drive her late husband, Morris, to distraction. It was like a horse charging around the room. She could alter the percussive pattern, and sometimes it sounded like a snare drum cadence. That one had especially annoyed Morris. He claimed the rhythm lingered in his mind the way a mention of familiar lyrics might get a song stuck in someone's head.

She decided to research people associated with the production but who didn't actually appear on stage. Like Sid. He had a sizeable, though not especially impressive, list of credits to his name. These easily surfaced during Google and Bing searches. Mitchell Morgan's name also brought up plenty of results. As a media professional, he'd managed to splash his presence all over the internet.

Sadie bookmarked pages for both the director and the publicist and moved on. Curious to find background information on the mysterious Nevada Foster, it made sense to turn to the person who had pushed to include her in the show to begin with.

The list of Ernie Palmer's business endeavors stretched several paragraphs on his Wikipedia page. Many, though not all, were theatre ventures, usually musical productions of medium size, neither Broadway-scale nor small town shows. He'd backed a profitable short run of *Seven Brides for Seven Brothers* in San Antonio, a staging of *The King and I* in Chicago, a month-long production of *Pippin* in Atlanta, and a flop of an original play in Miami, which had closed after the second night.

Ernie Palmer's name and accomplishments were well known. Newspapers and local talk shows often mentioned his numerous financial projects. He drew criticism from time to time for being somewhat of a braggart, though he'd had his fair share of business losses, as well as successes. But Sadie was less interested in his professional affairs than she was in his personal history. From what she'd observed, he seemed as concerned with Nevada personally as he was with the potential profit from production. Pushing for her to get the lead role, for example – was that really just a question of making money from the show? And his disapproval of her over-imbibing at the cast get-together – was he merely concerned for her reputation?

An online bio for Ernie showed him born in the Bronx to parents of modest means. He'd been an only child. Raised in New York for most of his childhood, the family moved to Chicago during his teen years. He finished high school there and enrolled in business classes at a community college. He'd been married briefly once to someone named Margaret Retsof, but divorced quickly. Both parents were deceased.

Sadie thought this over. No siblings, no spouse, no children, no living parents. It sounded lonely at first glance, though it wasn't unlike Sadie's own history, aside from the fact she was widowed. She'd gone on to run an established fashion boutique, as well as side forays into amateur detective escapades. Ernie had gone on to start small business endeavors, eventually moving on to larger projects, mostly investments, nothing personal.

So why the special interest in Nevada Foster? Sadie reminded herself not to read too much into every detail she discovered. Perhaps Nevada *was* simply a means to an end: money, Ernie's favorite thing.

Amber was in the process of signing for a UPS delivery when Sadie returned to the front of the store. Sadie smiled, knowing this would take a few minutes. Handsome and single, at least according to the absence of a ring on his left hand, the young driver always brought out Amber's flirtatious side. He responded to Amber by flirting back, though of course he had to excuse himself – reluctantly, it seemed – to return to his regular route.

"No date yet?" Sadie asked after the driver left.

"I'm working on it. I don't want to seem too eager."

"You could just ask him out, you know," Sadie suggested. "It's not like it used to be when I was your age."

"Sadie, knowing you, I doubt you would have hesitated." Amber laughed. "You don't follow the crowd. And I mean that in a good way." She reached for a box cutter.

"You're right," Sadie admitted. "I remember startling my first husband when I suggested we go to the movies. But it wasn't considered proper for a girl to be so forward then. No one cares now as long as someone gets the ball rolling."

"I'll think about it." Amber slit open the box and lifted out a flat stack of brightly colored T-shirts. "Ah, these are great. I remember when we found this designer at the last trade show." She held one up, a long-sleeved cornflower blue selection. On the front was an old-fashioned seed packet design, accented with rhinestones and glitter. "These will complement that new line of jeans we got in last week."

"And the jewelry from Bali that we have on order," Sadie added.

"Yes!" Amber replied. "I think I see a new front window arrangement on the horizon."

"Excellent idea," Sadie agreed. "I always love your displays. I'm sure that's part of the reason we see new customers all the time."

"The constant supply of chocolate doesn't hurt, either," Amber said.

"Of course not," Sadie laughed. "Shopping and chocolate, two of the finer things in life!"

CHAPTER SEVENTEEN

Sadie followed the newspaper and television reports over the next few days, dividing her time between tending the store and getting updates on Brynn Baker's murder. According to the media, there were no new leads. She stayed in touch with Roxy, but the only extra information she learned was that several cast members had been called in for questioning. No one else had been arrested or even named a suspect. Most went in willingly, though apparently Alex had put up a fuss, calling the session a pointless hassle, saying he needed to stay focused on the play. Even Penelope had been interrogated, though Sadie doubted the police heard much of the gossip the girl shared with Freda

This lack of new information made her eager to get back to Monterey to see what she could dig up. By Thursday morning, she knew she had to return to the scene of the crime, so to speak, to move her own investigation forward.

"Time to pack," Sadie said out loud as she folded up the Thursday morning newspaper and set it aside. Coco, who was curled up on the living room couch, head resting comfortably on her plush red lobster, stretched her limbs, yawned and relaxed back into her cushy position. She regarded Sadie with casual disinterest. It wasn't her job to pack, after all.

"I'll start with my suitcase. Remind me to leave room for things I might buy. We should clean out your tote bag, too. Might as well start fresh for this trip."

Sadie could have sworn she saw Coco frown as she stood and headed to her closet. The phrases "clean out" and "tote bag" weren't Coco's favorites. The Yorkie's habit of burying items in the bottom of the bag and hiding things in the interior pockets was, to the little dog, important. The mess in the tote wasn't all Coco's fault, of course. Sadie's own habit of stashing trinkets in the bag also added to the clutter. It was a good thing the tote was large and roomy, with plenty of pockets, and that Coco was tiny. It seemed there was always space for something else, just as there would be in a bottomless pit or black hole.

She selected several outfits from her wardrobe and arranged them in her suitcase, folded in a special way she had learned over the years to avoid wrinkles. Since she'd need to be backstage with Coco, and Roxy preferred only dark clothing, that's mostly what she packed. But there was no sense in looking disheveled, even if the lights would be low. She hung one nicer outfit in a wardrobe bag, something shimmery and silver that she could wear for the cast party. In a small jewelry case, she tucked a set of dangling star earrings – what could be more appropriate!

Sadie set her luggage by the front door and started in on the tote bag. Coco began to groom her paws with fixed concentration. Out came a show program, several flyers with Coco's photo, post cards of Monterey Bay, a hotel brochure, business cards from boutiques she'd visited, a spare charger for the tablet she carried when traveling, a roll of breath mints, wadded up scraps of paper with Coco's practice pawtographs, and a phone.

A phone?

She hadn't left her phone in the tote bag. In fact, she'd been using it all week, including the night before when she sent texts to both Roxy and Amber. She always set it down on a desk, table, or counter, when finished – never put it back in the bag. This wasn't the model of phone she owned, and it wasn't enclosed in her own stylish case.

She dropped the phone on the couch in shock, rather the way she dropped the annual property tax bill for her penthouse. Could this be Russell's phone? Panic washed over her. She had touched it; her fingerprints were on it. *Wipe them off,* she thought, but quickly stopped herself. What if the killer's prints were on there, too? Then she'd be destroying evidence.

"Oh, Coco. This is not good. This is *not* good at all!"

Coco let out an apologetic or defensive whine – most likely both. Sadie knew her tone of voice matched the one she'd used the time Coco had played with – that is, borrowed and buried – a diamond bracelet that had fallen off a lady's wrist at a charity event and landed on the floor beside the tote bag. Sadie had gone so far as to use the dreaded words, "Coco, no!" as she'd held up the sparkling piece of jewelry in dismay after she'd gotten home that evening. The bracelet's owner had been distraught when she'd realized it was missing at the gala. At the time, it hadn't occurred to Sadie to check her purse. It turned out that it was easier to explain what happened the next day than it would have been the night the bracelet went missing. The woman was so grateful to have her bracelet returned that she laughed and offered to buy Sadie a cup of coffee.

Frantic, Sadie began to pace back and forth. How was she going to explain this to Detective Higgins? He had yet to show one ounce of a sense of humor. She'd be facing a grim reprimand. Even worse, this situation would finger her as a suspect, wouldn't it? She'd certainly suspect herself, if she didn't already know she was innocent. How plausible was it going to sound to Higgins that Coco was behind this? *Was* Coco behind it? Maybe someone else dropped the phone into her bag to throw the police off. She got as close as she could to the device without touching it again and studied its screen. There was a familiar smear, something she recognized from the many times Coco had licked her phone when she happened to leave it lying too close to the Yorkie's level.

"I hope you didn't lick off all the fingerprints!" Sadie's thoughts careened in ridiculous directions. Coco wasn't the type of dog to wish anyone harm. She'd never shown any signs of aggression. She wasn't big enough or strong enough to push someone off a catwalk. And she couldn't have sent a text to Brynn; she didn't have opposable thumbs!

Calm down, Sadie told herself. *These are crazy thoughts.*

She was overreacting. This was just one piece of evidence in the murder case. *But it's the most important one!*

Sadie stared at the phone again. Maybe it was someone else's phone. Maybe she should check the text history to be sure. The police hadn't released the contents of the text someone had sent to Brynn, allegedly from Russell's phone, and Russell himself hadn't spilled that information to the bartender during the conversation Sadie overheard at the bar when he said he'd lost his phone.

The urge to read the texts won out over Sadie's practical thought of slipping the phone in a plastic bag and not touching it again until she turned it over to Higgins. A quick look at the most recent text confirmed the phone was Russell's. The text was to Brynn, and read, "Meet me tonight at the usual place," with a heart emoji after the period. Sadie dropped the phone again.

She fetched a plastic bag from the kitchen and set it beside the phone. *Russell's missing phone.* In her latest update, Roxy had told Sadie the police had yet to find the device. And now she knew why.

"Oh dear, Coco," Sadie blurted out. "I'm afraid you're an accessory to murder!"

Could a dog be charged? No, of course not. Sadie's thoughts were becoming muddled again. She took several deep breaths, which calmed her down temporarily, until the next realization hit. But *I* could be charged!

She would just have to explain her possession of the phone to Detective Higgins in a logical way, if only she could think what that might be. It would be easier to do if she had more information before she turned over the phone.

"Coco, the only way out of this is to solve the crime," Sadie said. Coco switched paws and continued her grooming session, never looking up.

The sound of an incoming phone call caused her to jump before she realized it was from her own phone, which rested innocently beside the morning paper.

I really need to get a grip, Sadie said to herself. She took another deep breath as she reached for the phone. Not surprisingly, it was Roxy.

"Good morning, more like afternoon," Roxy said. "Just checking to see when you'll be driving down. I'm having terrible cravings for potato skins."

Sadie remained silent, debating whether or not to tell Roxy about Russell's phone. She decided to wait. "I'm leaving soon. I'll text you when I get there."

"You sound shaky," Roxy said.

"I'm fine."

"You don't sound fine, Sadie. Are you sure you're OK?"

"Of course." Sadie could hear the lack of certainty in her own voice. "I've just made a small ... discovery, you might say." *Understatement of the century...*

"Oh, cool," Roxy said. "You found out something the police haven't discovered yet?"

"You might say that," Sadie said.

"Do tell!"

"I'll explain when I get there," Sadie said. "I'm almost done packing. I'll be there in a few hours."

Sadie ended the call and set her phone next to her car keys, not to confuse it with the more recent, unfortunate discovery. She opened up the plastic bag and attempted to slide one edge of it under Russell's phone, hoping to nudge it inside without touching it again. But as she pushed the slim plastic edge against the device, it simply moved forward instead of sliding inside. She changed strategy and held the plastic bag's edge firmly with both hands and pushed down against the couch's surface, attempting to bounce the phone slightly toward the bag's interior. This was equally unsuccessful. She finally picked up Coco and told her to "sit" on the couch and "stay." She then pushed the plastic bag against the phone, which, now blocked by Coco's paws, could not slide away. Within moments, the phone was bagged, the bag was sealed, and the evidence was safely tucked away.

Twenty minutes later, Sadie and Coco were on the way to Monterey.

CHAPTER EIGHTEEN

The hotel charmed Sadie just as much on this visit as it had the first time she'd stayed there. She even managed to score the same luxurious room. She could hardly wait until it was time to crawl under the heavenly linens, though she had hours to go before she could sleep. She made a mental note to find out what brand the sheets were so she could pick up a set for her penthouse.

It didn't take long for her to unpack her suitcase since she'd packed light with the intention of filling the extra space with things she knew she would buy in Carmel. She planned to hit Ocean Avenue, a spot that she rarely visited though it was only a short drive from San Francisco. It would be a shame to waste the opportunity.

Coco settled in just as easily, as if the plush surroundings were standard treatment for a star. The hotel concierge had even arranged a welcome basket of canine treats and toys with Coco's name on it, cleverly set on a plush dog bed, at just the right height for a Yorkie. The staff had also left a basket with human treats at desk level.

Sadie shot off a quick text to Roxy, letting her know she'd arrived, then, with Coco napping comfortably in her travel palace, left for The Sea Urchin. It was too early for Happy Hour, but the perfect time for a serving of chocolate lava cake and an espresso. She took her tote bag with her since she didn't want to leave the newly found evidence in the hotel room. Even without Coco's minor, extra weight, the bag felt heavy with the knowledge of what was inside.

As Sadie entered the bar and sat in a back booth, Roxy returned her text. *On my way*, it said.

"Welcome back. What can I get you?"

Sadie recognized the server, who also seemed to remember her from the previous weekend. She also recognized the bartender as the one who'd been on duty when she'd overheard Russell talking to him. Her fingertips tingled, as if they were about to feel their way to a few answers.

"Ma'am?"

"Oh, sorry," Sadie said, realizing her thoughts had kept her from giving her order. "I'd love an espresso, please, and a serving of chocolate lava cake."

"Coming right up."

"And," Sadie added quickly before the server walked away, "an order of your potato skins for a friend who's joining me. In fact, there she is."

Roxy, clad in jeans, boots and an oversized sweatshirt, ordered black coffee and sat down across from Sadie as the server walked away.

"I ordered potato skins for you," Sadie said, admiring a bejeweled bracelet Roxy wore, which looked strangely incongruous with the rest of her outfit.

"Perfect," Roxy said. "I haven't eaten all day, other than a toasted bagel eight hours ago."

"Busy? Even without a show tonight?"

Roxy shrugged. "Yes and no. Not so much busy as just frantic and frustrating. I've had constant interruptions, which makes it hard to get anything done."

"Detective Higgins still?" Sadie glanced around, as if she expected him to pop up at any moment.

"No, not the last couple of days, thank goodness," Roxy said. "He's called a few people down to the station for questioning, like I told you, but I don't think the theatre itself interests him anymore. They've searched it several times. They haven't found anything new."

She glanced at her tote bag nervously. How was she going to explain having Russell's phone, even to Roxy?

"You said Higgins called Alex in the other day," Sadie said, stalling for a moment. "But he resisted going in?"

Roxy shrugged. "He didn't resist. He just had an attitude about it."

"Why wouldn't he want to cooperate? That just makes him look guilty, don't you think?" Sadie paused as the server delivered the food and beverages, and watched as she walked away. She turned back toward Roxy. "Do you think Alex has something to hide?"

"Who knows?" Roxy said. "Maybe he does. Everyone knew he was sweet on Brynn."

"Then he'd be the last person to want to hurt her, right? Unless..." Sadie fell silent.

"Unless what?" Roxy asked. She reached for a potato skin, twisting it sideways as melting cheese dripped onto the serving plate.

"Unless he didn't want anyone else to have her," Sadie said. "Maybe he knew she was seeing Russell, and was jealous. You said they competed for her attention."

"True," Roxy said. "But to kill someone just so no one else could have that person? Seems extreme to me."

"Murder *is* extreme," Sadie pointed out, "whatever the reason behind it." She picked up a spoon and dug into the chocolate lava cake.

"So," Roxy continued, "spill it."

"Spill what?" Sadie took a sip of espresso and glanced at her tote bag again.

"You know," Roxy said. "The discovery you told me about earlier."

"Oh, that..." Sadie hesitated. Even though she knew Roxy well, she wasn't sure divulging the information about the phone was smart. Maybe she'd be better off going straight to the police and turning it in. And explaining...explaining what? That her dog was a kleptomaniac? How believable would that be?

"Sadie?" Roxy prompted.

Sadie took another bite of chocolate and debated her approach, finally deciding to just lay it all out, starting with the phone itself. She looked around the nearly empty bar and pulled the plastic bag from her tote. Setting it on the table, she watched Roxy frown.

"I don't understand," Roxy said. "Why do you have your cell phone in a plastic bag? Did you drop it in something? Are you trying to muffle the sound? You know phones can be set on vibrate." Roxy reached out for the bag, but Sadie stopped her.

"You won't want to touch that," Sadie said.

Roxy froze, her hand halfway to the questionable plastic bag. Slowly, she drew her arm back. "Why not?"

"Because it's not my phone," Sadie said, pulling her own phone out of a side pocket and holding it up.

"Not your phone? Then whose is it?" Roxy frowned, and then her eyes grew wide. "Oh, no, Sadie. Don't tell me."

Sadie nodded. "Yes, I'm afraid so. It's Russell's phone."

Roxy gasped. "How? Where? Are you sure?"

"Very sure," Sadie said. "It's obvious from the text history."

"You looked at the phone? You touched it? Your fingerprints are on it?" Roxy leaned forward, staring at the plastic bag.

Sadie waited until Roxy fell quiet to answer. "Yes, I looked at it and touched it. I had no idea it was Russell's until I'd already pulled it out of the tote bag. I didn't *decide* to handle it. I already had my hands on it when I realized what it was."

"How did it get..." Roxy sighed. "Never mind. I can figure that much out. You know, some people have toddlers who are easier to control than that Yorkie of yours."

"She just has that *joie de vivre*, you know," Sadie said in Coco's defense.

"That much is clear," Roxy said. "Anyway, what did the text history show?"

Sadie lowered her voice. "You remember the police said there was a text on Brynn's phone that made them suspect Russell, but they didn't release the content?"

"Yes," Roxy said.

"Well, here it is." Sadie lifted the plastic bag up and pushed the message icon, which brought up the last text.

Roxy's hand flew up and covered her mouth. "*Meet me tonight at the usual place*," she whispered. "Then it *was* Russell! Oh, this is terrible! And to think that he's running around loose – and back in the show, no less! Now we'll need to put Alex back in, which puts Coop back in..." Roxy held up fingers as she counted off steps she'd have to take before the next show.

"Hold on, Roxy." Sadie said, calming her friend with a gentle tap on her arm. "This doesn't prove anything. Remember Russell said he hadn't sent her a text. In fact, he claimed he'd lost his phone."

"But he could be lying," Roxy said.

"Yes," Sadie said. "But he could also be telling the truth. Anyone could have sent that text – anyone who had the phone, that is."

"It sort of looks like you had the phone," Roxy pointed out.

"That exact thought occurred to me," Sadie said. "Which is why we have to figure out who *did* have it that day."

"When was the text sent?" Roxy asked.

Both women leaned close to the phone, attempting to see through the plastic. Sadie adjusted the phone's angle, moving it to avoid glare from the bar lights, until she found a position that allowed them to read the date and time stamp.

"Five thirty-five the evening of the dress rehearsal," Roxy noted.

Sadie nodded. "Right. So it was before the rehearsal started at seven o'clock."

"But after the call time, which was five o'clock," Roxy said. "Which means Russell was already at the theatre, but so was everyone else. Just about anyone could have taken the phone and sent that text."

"Exactly," Sadie said. "In a way, that makes Russell look less guilty. He's only one of dozens of people who could have gotten ahold of his phone."

"True." Roxy nodded her head and reached for a potato skin.

"Who else would have been at the theatre that day?" Sadie took another sip of espresso and waited for Roxy's response.

"Anyone involved with the show," Roxy said. "You know, you were there. Penelope was working the box office, Freda was handling wardrobe, Coop was helping me, and Sid was running around barking at people, as usual."

"And Ernie and Mitchell were around, at least down at Curtain Call, where I saw them," Sadie said.

"They would have watched the dress rehearsal, too," Roxy said. "From the back row, their usual spot."

"That makes sense," Sadie mused. "Though I sat about halfway to the front and wouldn't have thought to look around the audience. So I can't say I saw them, except at the café."

Sadie finished off the chocolate lava cake and set the dish aside. She propped her chin in one hand and drummed her fingers on the tabletop with the other.

"Let's say Russell is innocent," Roxy said. Sadie suspected this was as much wishful thinking as it was an actual presumption. Roxy had already made it clear that she wasn't willing to accept that she'd have a killer running around during the performance.

"OK," Sadie said. "That means someone else took his phone in order to send the text. How would they get it?"

"That's easy," Roxy said. "Russell always left his phone sitting out on the dressing room table. Anyone could have grabbed it."

"Do you remember anyone in particular back there?" Sadie asked.

Roxy shook her head. "No, not really. I was moving around a lot before the rehearsal, all over the theatre, really, getting things ready."

"What about during the show?"

"I don't remember," Roxy said. "Wait, Ernie came back around intermission, but he just brought Nevada coffee."

"And that was long after the text was sent," Sadie pointed out.

"True," Roxy agreed. "I'll ask Coop if he remembers seeing anyone in or around Russell's dressing room earlier."

"In particular, before five thirty," Sadie added.

"Right." Roxy devoured the last potato skin. "Walk over to the theatre with me," Roxy said. "I want you to see the new flyers Mitchell made up for the show. The entire border is paw prints."

"Sure," Sadie said. She waved the server over and asked for the check. She signed the charge over to her hotel bill and followed Roxy out of the bar. Sadie took a detour to her room so she could gather up Coco, rather than leave her alone for an indefinite period of time. Who knew how long the police station visit would take?

She rejoined Roxy in the lobby, and the two walked down to the theatre, ending up just behind the stage, where Roxy had saved a stack of the new flyers for Sadie to keep.

"Oh, I love them!" Sadie exclaimed. She set her tote bag down and carried one of the papers over to inspect under the brighter stage lights. "The paw print border is fabulous."

"I knew you'd like them," Roxy said. "As annoying as Mitchell can be at times, he does come up with great publicity ideas."

"Just fabulous," Sadie repeated. "Don't you think so, Coco?" She turned the flyer toward the tote bag, which Coco was circling, as if on patrol. "Oh no, Coco," she said. "No more shenanigans from you." Placing the Yorkie back in the tote, she tucked a few of the papers in a side pocket and accompanied Roxy back outside.

"I'm off to run errands. What about you?"

Sadie managed a nervous laugh. "I believe I'm headed for a highly entertaining meeting with Detective Higgins."

"Good luck," Roxy said.

"Thanks," Sadie said. "I'll need it."

CHAPTER NINETEEN

The police station loomed before Sadie with much the same intimidating look as the theatre had when she first saw it. Even without gargoyles, the building elicited from her a sense of dread. Not that the sleek, modern exterior of the building resembled the theatre in any way. It was the anticipation of confessing Coco's crime that had her nerves in knots.

If her fingerprints hadn't been on the phone, she might have been tempted to drop it off anonymously. But her responsible decision to not tamper with evidence meant leaving her own prints on the phone, as well as any others. She just had to face up to being in possession of what was likely the most important missing clue. And hope she could explain it.

Sadie climbed the half dozen steps, entered the station, and approached a reception desk manned by two officers.

"I'd like to speak with Detective Higgins."

"What is this regarding?" The officer asking the question looked to be in her mid-thirties. She had short brown hair, neatly-manicured fingernails and a no-nonsense expression.

"It's...personal," Sadie said.

The officer exchanged looks with the second officer, an older man Sadie figured to be in his late forties. His expression led Sadie to interpret that by "personal," she meant *personal*.

"No," Sadie stammered. "That's not what I meant to say. I'd just like to speak with him personally."

"We can take a report here at the desk," the female officer said, "if you need to file one."

Sadie clutched the handles of her tote bag nervously. "I'd just like to speak with Detective Higgins, please. If he's here, that is. It's about the Brynn Baker case."

"What is your name?"

Sadie gave the officer her name and watched as he picked up a phone on the desk.

"Higgins, there's someone here to see you, a Sadie Kramer." He paused. "All right, I'll tell her to wait." He hung up the phone and turned back to Sadie. "Just take a seat. He'll be out in a few minutes."

"Thank you," Sadie said curtly. She silently reprimanded herself for being snippy. She wasn't really impatient with the desk officers. She was just apprehensive about talking to Higgins. "Thank you," she repeated, making a point of softening her voice.

Five minutes passed, during which Sadie hushed a whining Coco several times, observed ongoing business behind the desk, and did breathing exercises that she'd read about recently in a magazine, hoping that would calm her down. Still, she jumped when she saw Higgins emerge from a hallway and look her way.

"Ms. Kramer."

Sadie stood quickly, as if being summoned to a school principal's office. She reminded herself silently that she hadn't done anything wrong. She crossed her fingers around one of the tote handles. She hoped it would be clear that she was only there to help.

"Detective Higgins, it's nice to see you." The words had barely passed over her lips before she realized they were anything but true.

"What brings you in today?"

Sadie looked around before speaking. "I'd really like to talk with you in private."

"We can go into a room down the hall. I just need to let them search your bag before I take you back." He indicated the front desk. The female officer stood up and reached for the bag.

Sadie felt a wave of panic. "Is that really necessary?"

"Yes it is," Higgins said. "Do you have a problem with that?"

"Of course not," Sadie lied, knowing she had no other choice. As she handed over the tote, she comforted herself with the thought that people sometimes had two phones. Maybe it wouldn't seem strange when the bag was searched. Of course, there was always the other factor...

The female officer took on an expression of disdain when she took her first glance into the bag. She reached in reluctantly and lifted out the Yorkie as if handling toxic waste. She placed Coco on the desk. Her colleague raised his eyebrows. She then rifled through the bag. Apparently finding nothing forbidden, she deposited Coco back in the tote and handed it to Sadie, who breathed a sigh of relief.

"Follow me." Higgins turned away and led Sadie to a small room, offered her a chair and sat down across from her. Saying nothing, he waited for Sadie to speak.

Sadie shifted her position several times, and then finally said, "I brought you something." She reached into the tote bag. Coco whined softly as Sadie slipped her hand slowly into an interior pocket, then more rapidly into another, and yet another. Her heart began to race. "I have it...sorry, Detective Higgins, just give me a moment." Coco began whining louder as Sadie pulled her out of the bag and set her on the interview table, and continued to rummage frantically through the tote. Where was the phone?

"Ms. Kramer?"

Sadie looked up to see that Coco was lavishing kisses on the detective's neck, a good distraction from her confusion. *Good dog!* she thought.

"Coco, get down," Sadie said. "You know better than to climb on people."

Coco obeyed and jumped down. She curled up on the table and watched Sadie and Higgins.

"I'm sorry about that." Sadie smiled sheepishly. "She does love a man with a badge!" One by one, she pulled items out of the tote bag and placed them on the table while continuing her search: the show flyers, silver bangles, bright purple sunglasses, cherry-flavored lip gloss, a hotel room key, and several other items. If she hadn't cleaned the tote out before she returned to Monterey, the process would have taken even longer.

"What exactly are you looking for?" The detective was running out of patience.

"I thought I brought you..." Sadie paused. How could she say she had Russell's phone and then not produce it? She had to think quickly. "I thought I brought...a list of questions, no, more like ideas about Brynn Baker's murder. But I can't seem to find it now." *Of course I can't find it, since it doesn't exist...* She glanced at Coco, as if she could somehow help her out of the tight spot. She could almost swear the Yorkie raised an eyebrow in amusement. *You're no help,* she thought.

Detective Higgins leaned forward, though slightly away from Coco. "What sort of ideas?"

"Well, I don't know without the list." Sadie attempted to sigh nonchalantly, which sounded more like choking on an oversized chunk of cucumber.

"I see."

"I must have left it at the hotel," Sadie said, standing up in what she hoped was a casual manner, rather than revealing her urge to flee the building. "I wish I could remember what I jotted down. But, you know, at my age my memory isn't what it was. I'll try to find the list and bring it by later on today, or maybe tomorrow morning."

"I would appreciate that," Higgins said. He sounded like he wasn't sure the list existed. Probably, he thought she had no ideas, and possibly nothing much at all between her ears. *Better to be thought an airhead than a criminal.*

Detective Higgins escorted Sadie back to the station entrance, where Coco popped her head out of the bag to give the female officer at the front desk something resembling a stink eye.

"You'll let me know if you find your list, all right?" Higgins said politely.

"Of course," Sadie said as she backed out the door. "Always happy to help!"

* * *

Sadie parked her car on Carmel's Dolores Street and walked back to Ocean Avenue. If she hadn't been ready for retail therapy earlier, she certainly was now. The meeting with Detective Higgins had been not only unproductive, but also downright ridiculous.

A splash of chartreuse in a store window caught Sadie's eye, and she ducked into a quaint boutique with a curlicue sign above the door. With a few gyrations undoubtedly unbecoming for a woman her age, she managed to peer through the backdrop of the display to identify the item in question: a soft knit poncho in a green-yellow color that several of her own customers found disturbing, yet she'd always loved.

"May I help you find something?"

The voice sounded familiar, but Sadie couldn't place it until she turned around and found herself face to face with Freda, the wardrobe supervisor from the Seaside Players.

"Well, hi there!" she said. "It's Coco's mom."

"Hello, Freda. Moonlighting at this boutique?"

"Not exactly moonlighting" Freda said. "I've worked here for years. Usually full time, but only part time when the theatre has a production going on." She looked over Sadie's shoulder, into the front display. "Something in the window you'd like to see?"

"That poncho," Sadie said, indicating the bright article of clothing.

Freda pointed to a rack along the side of the store, and led Sadie to it. "We have those over here. They come in several colors, including the one in the window. They're from Peru, an alpaca wool blend. One size fits all."

"That's the best part about ponchos!" Sadie exclaimed. "One size *does* fit all. Always a little room for a few extra desserts, if you know what I mean!" Sadie patted a hip enthusiastically with one hand, the tote bag swinging on the opposite arm from the movement. A faint whine came from inside.

"Hush!" Sadie whispered.

"I beg your pardon?" Freda raised an eyebrow.

"Oh, not you!" Sadie said, her face flushing. "That was for Coco. She prefers a smoother ride." Sadie held the tote open to reveal Coco curled up in its bottom.

Freda dipped her hand into the bag and rubbed between Coco's ears. "How's our little angel doing?"

"She's doing great. She thrives on the attention and loves to travel. She also loves to shop."

"I see," Freda said. "Such a little love. She must be a great companion."

Sadie nodded and reached out to touch the closest poncho, admiring the soft texture of the weave. "I love this peachy color, too."

"That's called salmon sunset. It's been very popular." Freda pulled the poncho from the rack and hung it face out. She did the same with the chartreuse version, letting Sadie see them side by side. "The matching blouses make it easy to pull a smart look together," she added, pointing to another section on the same rack. "Lighter shades of the same colors."

"I can see those blend in nicely," Sadie said, then paused. "Such a shame about the murder," She stood back to admire the full collection of garments and compare the chartreuse and salmon colors. "What a terrible shock for you all."

"Yes, an awful shock," Freda said. "Though it was a ridiculous meeting place they had, don't you think, the catwalk? Penelope and I were just talking about that the other day."

"Meeting place?" Sadie asked. Her pulse quickened in anticipation of new information.

"Yes, Brynn and Russell. Apparently they'd been meeting there," Freda said. "At least that's what Penelope told me, that she'd seen them up there after hours. She cleans the theatre at night sometimes, you know."

Sadie tipped her head to the side, keeping her eyes on the clothing in order to appear nonchalant about the tidbit of gossip. "That's right. Well, I agree, it's an odd place to meet. But I'm not crazy about heights, so it wouldn't be my choice, in any case."

"Not mine either," Freda said. "So, would you like to try on one of the ponchos?"

Sadie reached out and lifted the hangers, one in each hand, resulting in another faint whine from her tote bag. "No need. One size fits all, right? I'll take them both, plus blouses to match. Better make those a large … er, extra large, maybe."

"Excellent." Freda smiled as she pulled the items from the rack. "I'll help you out up front."

At the cash register, Sadie pulled out her wallet and gave Freda her credit card. She signed the store copy of the charge receipt and watched as Freda folded the items inside tissue paper and placed them in an elegant fuchsia bag with silver ribbons for handles.

"Personally," Freda said, leaning forward across the counter as she handed Sadie the bag, "I think Russell did it."

"Why do you think Russell might have wanted to kill Brynn?" Sadie asked. 'I don't know him at all, but if he and Brynn were secretly dating, it seems strange for him to want to kill her. Unless they had some kind of fight?'

"That missing phone story? Too convenient, don't you think?" Freda said. She straightened up and twisted her stud earring while she waited for Sadie's reply.

"I don't know," Sadie said, admiring the bright bag as an excuse to avoid eye contact. "People do lose phones. And they pick up other people's phones by accident, since so many look alike these days."

"Well, I say if that phone shows up, they'll know who did it," Freda said. "Maybe they already know. The police don't release all the information to the public. They might even have the phone already. In any case, it must be around somewhere."

"It just might be," Sadie said. "You never know."

CHAPTER TWENTY

Coco batted a circular makeup puff up off the dressing room table, flipping it onto her head like a hat. Flurries of talc floated downward, showering her in a thin layer of powder.

"Coco!" Sadie reprimanded the Yorkie and apologized to Freda, who had turned away momentarily from the task of dressing Coco to grab a hair clip.

"It's fine." Freda sighed, removed the puff and brushed the powder out of Coco's fur before placing the sequined bow on her head.

"She's just amped up," Sadie offered. "All this activity! And so many of the cast and crew welcoming her back with hugs and treats."

It wasn't difficult for Sadie to explain; she felt the same way. Being backstage again brought back all the thrill of the previous weekend, minus the tragic aspect of Brynn Baker's murder. Now, two shows remained, both sold out. And then there was the cast party. Yes, it would be an exciting weekend for sure.

"Well, your little star is as ready as she'll ever be," Freda said. "I need to go check Russell's costume, make sure nothing was left askew when Alex wore it last weekend." She stepped back, eyed Coco's bow with satisfaction, and left the room.

"All's well?" Roxy popped her head into the room as soon as Freda stepped out.

"... that ends well, right?" Sadie silently patted herself on the back, though for no specific reason, since she couldn't accurately place the reference. Still, it sounded clever, considering the theatre setting.

"Yes," Roxy said. "All's well that ends well, as Shakespeare would say."

Aha! Sadie thought. *Shakespeare, of course.* "Yes, exactly. One of his comedies, right?"

"I suppose so," Roxy said. "At least it's classified as such. It's more of a problem play, really. Comedic elements, yet dark aspects. Several of his plays fall into that category."

"Sort of like *Songs to the Sun?*" Sadie said. It seemed appropriate, considering the odd mix of tragedy and comedy.

"I guess so," Roxy said. "Though the dark elements aren't part of this show. And we owe the comic features to Coco."

"You hear that?" Sadie scratched the Yorkie under her chin. "You're providing the comedy for this show." Coco tipped her head slightly to the side. The yip that followed sounded remarkably like "yep."

"I'll stop by the prop table after you get settled there. I have your headset, and Coop has the picnic basket." Roxy ducked back out of the room.

"OK, Coco, let's go. It's almost show time." Sadie reached out to pick Coco up, but didn't need to. Coco jumped down from the dressing table and trotted right out the door and straight to the prop area, proving she knew the backstage setup perfectly already. She hopped up on the table, nudged the edge of the picnic basket's lid with one paw in order to flip it open, and jumped in. Grasping a cluster of plastic grapes between her teeth, she curled up, ready for her performance.

"So this is the new little star," a deep voice said.

Sadie turned to see Russell standing beside the prop table. He looked as calm and collected as he had the night of the dress rehearsal, when Sadie had first seen him on stage. His hair was perfectly coifed, his costume was immaculate, and he didn't seem either stressed or guilt ridden. He was hardly anything like the rattled and tipsy man she saw at the bar the last weekend. Perhaps he'd already gotten over the arrest and Higgins' repeated questioning through the week. Either he was truly innocent and had nothing to be worried about, or he was an actor worthy of a much more complicated role than that in this play.

"Yes," Sadie said. "Coco, this is Russell. Russell, meet Coco. Russell reached one hand into the basket, just close enough for Coco to give it a sniff. Coco sneezed and dropped the grapes. She didn't seem to like Russell the way she adored Nevada or even Alex, but she didn't seem to find fault with him, either .

"I've never been much of a dog person, sorry," Russell said. He sounded polite yet non-apologetic.

"I have to say, I'm so impressed at your calm after all the police have put you through. If it were me, I'd be a mess," Sadie said.

"Well, I'm not guilty of anything, so once I got over the shock of being arrested, I had no reason to worry, you know. I decided to file the experience away so that I could call on it in the future if I ever play a criminal." His eyes skimmed Sadie's face, and he looked into the picnic basket at Coco again. "See you later, little dog." He gave her a perfunctory pat on the back. She bared her teeth but didn't snarl. Russell smiled and excused himself.

"Coco," Sadie whispered. "You could at least be polite and pretend to like people when you meet them. These *are* your coworkers now, you know."

Coco licked one paw, then ran it across her cheek and eyebrow, barely tapping the bow on her head.

"Watch out," Sadie warned. "You don't want Freda having to come back to redo your costume." Sadie checked the bow to make sure it was still secure, then saw Nevada approaching. "Oh, here comes one of your favorite people now, Coco."

Nevada swooped in like a fairy godmother, cupping Coco's delighted face between her hands and placing a light kiss on her forehead. "I just adore this dog!" she exclaimed to Sadie.

"The feeling is obviously mutual," Sadie said. She watched as Coco retrieved a leaf from inside the picnic basket and offered it to Nevada.

"Not yet, Coco," Nevada cooed. "Save that for the picnic scene. I'll be right there to help you. Sadie will tell you when to give me something."

Coop came by to give Sadie the headset sent by Roxy and to test it against the speaker in the basket. All passed inspection.

Sid zoomed through the backstage area briefly. "Good show, everyone!"

Ernie flagged Nevada down to hand her a bottle of water, and then insisted on placing it in her dressing room after she'd taken a quick drink.

"Places," Roxy called over the general headsets to the full cast.

Sadie watched as cues were called and the show began. Scene by scene unfolded during the first act. With Russell and Alex back in their regular roles, Coop was back at his role as Roxy's assistant, leaving Sadie with Coco as her sole charge. It felt slightly anti-climactic after all the hubbub of the previous weekend, yet she did on one occasion offer antiseptic spray to a stagehand who had picked up a splinter in one finger. This produced a burst of pride in Sadie over her recently acquired stagehand skills.

The picnic scene came and went without unusual incidents. Coco followed cues perfectly – after all, it was her third performance. She enchanted the audience by delivering grapes to Nevada, a tangerine to Alex, who thanked Coco with a muffled sneeze, a paper napkin to Russell – though only after repeated encouragement from Sadie – and a peach rose to Nevada, which Coco must have swiped from a dressing room delivery and stored before the lights came up. The audience didn't seem to care what item emerged from the picnic basket, or which recipient Coco chose. Just the presence of the petite cast member thrilled ticketholders. The curtain for intermission fell to thunderous applause.

"Great job," Roxy said once Sadie and Coco were back in the dressing room.

"I thank you, and Coco thanks you," Sadie said.

Roxy paused to answer a question in the hallway, and then turned back to Sadie. "I've got to be alert for when intermission ends. Staying back here for the second act?"

Sadie looked at Coco, who was stretched out on her back, upper torso headed one direction, lower torso in the other. Her eyes were closed and a miniature snore drifted upwards.

"I don't think so," Sadie said. "I'll take Coco back to the hotel to rest for a few minutes before we come back for the pawtograph signing. I wouldn't mind putting my feet up, either."

"I don't blame you at all," Roxy said. "And join us at Curtain Call later, too. It should be interesting with Russell back in the mix. He seems to think he's twice the star he was before, now that he's added his fifteen minutes of police fame to his acting credits."

"Unless those fifteen minutes of police fame actually *belong* on his resume," Sadie said.

Roxy raised both eyebrows.

"I'm not saying they do," Sadie added. "And don't worry. I'll be at the café later. I just need a little time at the hotel first. Maybe I'll change into something not quite as dark, for one thing." She chuckled as she delivered the last line. Roxy knew full well that black was not Sadie's usual color choice. She saw no need to dress like a stagehand when she wasn't playing the part of one.

* * *

The hotel was quiet when she returned, especially for a Friday night, but this didn't surprise her. The desk clerk had told her that quite a few guests were there specifically to see the show's last weekend run. Since it was intermission, they would be gathering in the lobby for drinks, rather than returning to their accommodations.

"Something's bothering me, Coco," Sadie said, once back in their room. "I just can't place my finger on what it is." She placed Coco in her portable palace, and then threw off the dark outfit she'd worn backstage. She pulled one of the new blouses from the closet, thankful she'd hung the new purchases that afternoon when she returned from shopping in Carmel. Donning a new poncho and her favorite rhinestone jeans, she brushed her hair out, admiring its current bottle red shade, and clipped it up with a seashell barrette that she'd found in the hotel gift shop.

"I still don't think Russell is the killer," Sadie continued, "though it's hard to tell without knowing whose fingerprints are on the phone." She glanced sideways at Coco, as if the Yorkie might simply tell her where the missing phone was. The picnic basket role in the play had only encouraged Coco's habit of hiding items and moving them around. "Oh, my! Coco!" Sadie said suddenly. "I certainly hope you didn't give that phone to anyone else! Not with my fingerprints on it!" She took a deep breath and told herself not to panic. That would be easy enough to explain. *Wouldn't it?*

Coco scratched her chin with a back paw and then settled against her stuffed red lobster, closing her eyes.

"You're absolutely no help," Sadie added.

Coco yawned.

"It could be Alex," Sadie murmured, aware she was only talking to herself at this point. "Jealousy over Brynn's attention to Russell, plus wanting that lead role. Maybe he was the person Coop heard yelling at Brynn in her dressing room. And he might have 'borrowed' Russell's phone…"

Sadie sat in the overstuffed chair and thought for a minute. Of course, if Alex had been the one to send the text, this would mean he knew Brynn and Russell's habit of meeting on the catwalk after hours. This was quite possible, now that she knew from Freda that Penelope could have mentioned that to anyone. But there was an inherent problem with that exact theory. Penelope *could* have mentioned it to *anyone*. Therefore, *anyone* could have known it would be easy to lure Brynn to the catwalk.

"Let's go, Coco," Sadie said. She stood up and retrieved her favorite gold flats from the closet, slipping them on her feet. Rousing Coco from her brief nap, she headed back to the theatre for the post-show pawtograph session.

* * *

"Love that color!" Roxy exclaimed as Sadie entered Curtain Call. "I wanted to tell you when I saw you at the pawtograph table, but you had quite a crowd there."

Sadie flipped her shoulders back and forth in a miniature shimmy at the compliment. "It's called 'salmon sunset' – divine, isn't it?"

The scene at the café was lively, but not chaotic. Coop leaned against a wall, a bottle of beer in one hand. Alex, Russell and Nevada sat together, chatting. Ernie hovered nearby, presumably watching Nevada to make sure she didn't drink too much.

"Fairly calm tonight," Sadie said as she looked around.

"I'm not surprised," Roxy said. "There's still one last show. Everyone will want to make it the best it can be. I'd expect a rowdier crowd at the cast party, though."

Sadie nodded. "Makes sense to me. I don't see Sid or Mitchell."

"They don't always come around after a show," Roxy said. "Ernie's here, but that's not unusual. He keeps a close eye on his little protégé."

"Trying to keep her in line?"

"Undoubtedly," Roxy said. "She seems to be on good behavior tonight, though."

"No sign of Higgins?"

Roxy shook her head. "I saw him at the theatre briefly, but he's not here. Maybe he finally got tired of questioning the same people. I know they're all tired of being grilled."

"I'm sure," Sadie murmured.

"Hey," Roxy said suddenly. "You never told me what happened when you turned in Russell's phone yesterday."

"Well, about that..." Sadie paused as Coop walked up.

"I'm calling it an early night," Coop said. "Not much going on. I want to rest up for tomorrow." With a quick wave, he headed out the door.

Sadie saw that the crowd was already thinning. Russell remained, wrapped up in a flirtatious conversation with a café worker who was clearly a fan. Alex had his jacket on already. Ernie was helping Nevada into a fluffy pink sweater.

"About the phone," Roxy prompted.

"Yes, well, that didn't go exactly as planned," Sadie said.

Roxy frowned and lowered her voice. "Well, you're not in jail, so it couldn't have gone too terribly wrong."

"You do have a point there," Sadie said. "But the truth is, it didn't go at all."

"What exactly does *that* mean?" Roxy said.

"It means when I reached in to pull it out of my bag, it wasn't there."

"What? Then where is it?"

"I have no idea," Sadie said. "But I hope it turns up soon."

CHAPTER TWENTY-ONE

"Coco!"

Sadie hugged the squirming Yorkie against her chest. Coco often got wound up around a lot of activity, but she was in unusually high gear. It almost seemed she knew this to be her last performance, and she meant to live it up to the fullest. She'd already escaped from the dressing room a few times, once ending up on Nevada's dressing table, begging for treats, and a second time she found her way to the lighting booth, where she'd delivered Freda's cloth tape measure to a very confused technician. Someone had even spotted her at the pawtograph table at one point, which fortunately hadn't been stocked yet with ink.

"You've got to calm down, Coco," Sadie whispered. She stroked the spot just above Coco's nose, a calming technique that had worked in the past.

"Is this going to be a problem?"

Sadie lifted her head at Sid's stern voice.

"Not at all, I assure you," Sadie said, hoping she'd be able to keep this promise. "She's just getting into character."

Sid grumbled something under his breath and stomped away, pausing to bark commands into several dressing rooms before leaving the backstage area.

Coop passed by, stopping to hand an extension cord to a stagehand before moving on.

"Thirty minutes to curtain." Roxy announced.

"Coco, I think a walk outside is in order for you," Sadie said. "Let's use up a little more of that energy before you take your place in the picnic basket." She pulled a rhinestone leash from the tote bag and clipped it to the Yorkie's collar, taking care not to disturb the sequined bow that Freda had already repositioned several times.

"Back in five," Sadie said in response to a concerned look on Roxy's face as she spotted Sadie and Coco heading for the stage door.

"Four," Roxy cautioned.

"Deal," Sadie said.

The fresh air in the alley revived Sadie after all that time she'd spent shuffling after Coco inside the theatre. Along with giving Coco a chance to burn off some excess energy, Sadie welcomed the break before the intensity of the final show. She strolled with Coco to the end of the alley where she could see the front of the theatre.

Crowds of theatregoers gathered on the steps, some dressed casually, others decked out for the special occasion. A line at the box office indicated customers picking up will-call tickets. Mitchell conversed with a young man holding a camera, likely a reporter, based on Mitchell's broad grin. Ernie stood to the side, talking on his cell.

Then Sadie spotted Detective Higgins. Unfortunately, he spotted her, too, before she could turn Coco back toward the stage door. He approached immediately, as she knew he would.

"Ms. Kramer."

"Detective Higgins." Sadie tried to sound casual, but winced when her voice squeaked.

"I don't suppose you ever came across that list you were looking for?"

Sadie shrugged. "I never did find it. I'm just terrible about keeping track of things, especially when I'm traveling. I probably threw it away by accident or lost it between here and San Francisco. Serves me right for scribbling ideas on scratch paper."

"I see," Higgins said. "It's curious that you found it important enough to bring the list to me at the station."

"Well, I must have thought it was important at the time, but I've forgotten the details, and the list is just gone," Sadie said. "I'm so sorry to have wasted your time that day." Sadie knew she was babbling. "I've been pretty scattered lately, what with Coco's newfound stardom and all the back and forth, you know?" Sadie glanced down the alley at the stage door. "I really do have to get back inside. The curtain rises soon." Coco tugged on the leash, as if to back up Sadie's statement.

"I understand," Higgins said. "Let me know if you happen to remember anything. Or, for that matter, if you see anything backstage that might be of help. You're in a unique position, you know. You're part of the show but also enough of an outsider to be objective."

"Absolutely," Sadie said. She returned to the stage door with Coco and stepped inside.

Coop spotted Sadie and Coco as they hurried up the stairs. "Glad you're back," he said as he handed her a headset. "Roxy was panicking. Fifteen minutes to curtain."

"Fifteen minutes," Sadie repeated, feeling quite the pro by this time. "We'll be ready."

Sadie settled into a chair beside the prop table and set Coco in her lap. Together they watched the last minute preparations.

Freda rushed by with a costume piece, a bandana that had gone missing, but had been found in the wings. Sadie looked at Coco and raised an eyebrow. Coco tipped her head innocently to the side.

"Places!" Roxy's voice came through Sadie's headset.

A rush of excitement ran through Sadie. This was it, the last show! She looked at her canine friend. "You'll be great, Coco," she whispered. "Everyone loves you."

Alex walked by, taking a place in the closest wing. He sneezed and cast a look at them.

"Well, almost everyone," Sadie amended, patting Coco's back.

One scene after another, the first act progressed. Enthusiastic applause floated back from the packed house.

"Warning picnic scene," Roxy called.

Coop stepped up to the prop table and held the picnic basket open as Sadie put Coco inside. As Coop took the basket out to the stage area and positioned it for the scene, Sadie followed and stood beside Roxy .

"Standby picnic scene." Roxy looked at Sadie and smiled. Sadie adjusted her headset and inhaled deeply.

"Go lights."

The spotlight focused on the picnic basket, highlighting the popping movement of the lid as Coco pushed against it from inside. Alex flipped the lid back, and rubbed his hands together in front of his face as if happy about the picnic lunch, but disguising his twitching nose.

"*Fluffy!*" Nevada cooed just as Coco's head popped up.

Applause filled the theatre before Coco even jumped out of the basket. The clapping turned to roaring laughter as Coco climbed out hind feet first, a maneuver that even took Sadie by surprise. *Where did she come up with that?* Sadie wondered, almost forgetting to give Coco her command.

"Give toys, Coco," Sadie said.

Coco pulled the plastic grapes from the basket and delivered them to Nevada. Encouraged by a warm hug of thanks from her favorite cast member, Coco ran back to the basket and jumped inside, landing in a way that showed only her wagging tail above the basket's rim. More applause from the audience.

Coco gave Alex the next gift, a paper cup, which he offered to Russell. Repeatedly, Coco returned to bring out other goodies: a wooden spoon, a large cookie, a banana, a plastic daisy, a small bag of potato chips. Nevada received the most gifts, but shared them around.

Sadie continued to issue the "give toys" command as the audience lapped up Coco's shenanigans. Just as it seemed time to wrap up the continuing parade, Coco jumped out with a plastic bag and walked toward the front of the stage.

She swung the bag from side to side, gripping it between her teeth.

"Not a sandwich again!" Coop whispered to Roxy and Sadie. "I warned the cast about keeping food around."

"It looks too heavy to be a sandwich," Roxy said, covering the mouthpiece to her headset.

Sadie gasped. "Oh my!" She pressed her fingers to her lips.

"What?" Roxy said.

Before Sadie could answer, the plastic bag broke open, and a clunky object slid across the wooden surface and came to rest just inches from the edge of the stage.

"It's a cell phone," Coop said. "Could it be...?"

"Oh, *Fluffy*, I believe that gift is for me." Russell jumped up faster than Sadie had seen him move yet. He lunged forward and reached for the phone, almost grabbing it before an arm stopped him.

"No, I actually believe that's for *me*."

Detective Higgins stood in front of the stage. He held Russell's arm with one hand and picked up the cell phone with the other. Confused, the audience laughed, assuming the unexpected interaction was simply part of the show.

Just before the curtain came down, in a move that Sadie could hardly believe, Higgins turned to Coco and said, "Thank *you*, Fluffy."

CHAPTER TWENTY-TWO

When Sadie entered Curtain Call, she saw that the cast and crew were decked out for the party, cocktails in hand, smiles plastered on faces. But the tension in the room was palpable. Even the shimmery sequined gown Sadie had changed into between the post-show pawtograph session and the cast party was not enough to douse her apprehension. There was an elephant in the room, an unexpected guest at what was supposed to be a celebration.

Roxy stood by the open bar, Coop with her. She waved Sadie over.

"No sign of Higgins yet?" Sadie said, accepting a champagne glass from a caterer.

Roxy shook her head and leaned closer to Sadie. "No. And you can tell people are nervous. After all, he did leave to run fingerprints during intermission. Anyone could have touched that phone."

"Plenty of theories being tossed around," Coop said. "At least half believe Russell is guilty. I can't say I disagree. You saw the way he rushed to get his hands on the phone."

"Really, Coop," Roxy said, "can you blame him? After all this time with the phone missing? *His* phone? Wouldn't you want to get it back if you were in his shoes?"

"Sure, if I thought it would suggest I was guilty," Coop said. "But then what would he have done with it, anyway? It's not like he could just hide it right there on the stage. Or make a run for it with so many people around."

Sadie sipped her champagne and watched the crowd. Many crew members had simply arrived in their backstage attire and aimed mainly for the food and drinks. Nevada had changed into a sweet silk outfit in pale pink that made her look more like a prom queen than a suspect. Alex wore jeans and a denim shirt, sleeves rolled up just enough to show off a pricey watch and muscled forearms. Nevada kept stroking his wrist.

"I take it Russell's down at the station again," Sadie said.

"You'd better believe it." Roxy sighed. "That's why we had to sub Alex back into Russell's role in the second act. Not that he minded a little extra exposure."

"Speaking of..." Coop murmured, barely audible to Sadie and Roxy. The three watched Alex saunter up to pick up two glasses of champagne, one for himself, and one for Nevada.

"Can you believe it?" Alex said. "Russell guilty after all?" He sipped from one glass and raised the other in Nevada's direction.

Sadie noticed Ernie, who leaned against a wall alongside Mitchell and Sid, frown as he watched Alex signal the incoming champagne to Nevada. *Still monitoring her behavior,* Sadie thought to herself. She wondered, suddenly, if Ernie was jealous of Nevada's affection for Alex. Maybe she was more to him than a potentially profitable protégé.

"I wouldn't jump to conclusions, Alex," Sadie ventured. "Just because Higgins took Russell in with him doesn't mean he's guilty. His fingerprints are probably on the phone, anyway. After all, it *is* his phone. I think what the detective is looking for is who else might have prints on the phone." She pulled Coco out of her tote bag and held her up. "I'd almost bet these little prints will show up."

"As if they'd have paw prints on file," Roxy laughed.

"Good point," Sadie admitted. "Let's just hope these paws and that little tongue didn't smear off other clues."

"Well, I'm not worried about Russell," Alex said. "If he did it, I'm glad they caught him. If he didn't do it, I hope they

catch the jerk that did. Brynn didn't deserve to die that way."
He headed back to sit with Nevada.

Sadie noticed Freda and Penelope hunched over a generous tray of appetizers, mouths in motion with food and chatter.

"Gosh," Sadie said. "I just realized I didn't eat much tonight. I'm going to swipe a couple of stuffed mushrooms from over there." She nodded toward the likely gossip zone and soon joined the table. To her delight, Freda and Penelope kept right on talking as if she weren't there.

"I say Nevada did it," Penelope said. "Just to get the lead part. You know how badly she wanted it. And I'm pretty sure she couldn't stand Brynn. I wouldn't put it past her."

"That's ridiculous," Freda said. "You wanted the part, too. But you didn't push Brynn off the catwalk to get it."

"I wasn't the understudy," Penelope pointed out, shrugging.

Sadie gawped at the tacky comment. It almost sounded like Penelope would have considered the drastic move, had she been in line for the role.

An unexpected hush came over the room, and Sadie turned around in her chair to see that Detective Higgins had just entered. Everyone stared at him. Cast members and crew lowered drinks from their lips, setting them on tables or counters. Nevada straightened her skirt; Mitchell, Sid and Ernie, all still leaning against the wall, seemed to stiffen. Even Penelope and Freda stopped talking.

Higgins turned down an offer of champagne and scanned the faces in the crowd. Not for the first time in her life, Sadie wished she could read minds. He was searching for someone; the question was who?

Russell stepped in behind him, snagged a glass of champagne, walked to a nearby table and sat. He chugged the champagne and wiped his mouth with the back of his hand. Sadie saw Freda lean toward Penelope and whisper, "I guess that rules out Russell." To which Penelope replied, "My money's still on Nevada."

"Twenty bucks says you're wrong," Freda quipped.

"You're on," Penelope said.

"I'd like everyone's attention," Higgins said, as if he didn't already have it. "We ran fingerprint tests on the *ever* so elusive cell phone that Fluffy was finally able to produce."

"It's *Coco*," Sadie whispered under her breath. Penelope, hearing her, actually giggled, which struck Sadie as completely out of character for someone who moments ago had seemed capable of throwing someone off a catwalk.

Coco heard her name, stuck her head out of the tote bag and looked around. Apparently sensing the tension in the room, she ducked quickly back inside. *Relax, Coco,* Sadie thought. *We already know your prints are on it.*

"We did find several sets of prints," Higgins continued. Sounds of shuffling and murmuring circled the room. "To start with, Sadie Kramer's fingerprints were on the phone."

The multitude of looks Sadie received included a look of sympathy from Roxy. Even though Sadie had shown her the phone the day she returned from San Francisco, Roxy must have thought the public announcement to be humiliating for Sadie, and downright perplexing for everyone else.

"We also found...well, I wouldn't call it exactly a print," Higgins said. "More like a smudge that I believe has a canine origin." He glowered at Sadie. "At least it matches the smudge on those flyers given out after the show."

"Those are *pawtographs*," Sadie said, quite irked to hear Coco's personal autograph referred to as a smudge.

Higgins hesitated, as if contemplating his next statement.

"Just tell us," Penelope said, impatient for what might be the best gossip of the year. Others echoed Penelope's demand.

Sadie surveyed the room, curious to see if anyone seemed especially nervous or more anxious than the others. Both Alex and Nevada were wearing what Sadie thought of as decent poker faces, but most of the people in the crowd appeared merely curious.

"We only found one other set of prints," Higgins continued, "and they're confusing since they don't belong to anyone associated with this play or the theatre, at least as far as we know." He paused long enough that Sadie wondered if it was simply for dramatic effect. On the other hand, he seemed to be studying people for their reactions.

Higgins pulled a notepad from his pocket and flipped the cover open. "Is anyone here familiar with Sarah Retsof?" He only got shrugs and shaking heads. He looked back at his notes. "She's in the system, with a record for petty theft."

"Is she wanted by the authorities?" Penelope sounded almost giddy, just at the thought of the fodder this would provide.

"No," Higgins said. "Not now. This is a past record, time served long ago. Yet her prints are on the cell phone, so she must have been around here. Does anyone have an idea why that would be?"

Sadie sat up straighter as the pieces fell together. She watched as the expressions on the cast and crew members shifted. Russell looked relieved, knowing he was finally in the clear. Both Penelope and Freda appeared disappointed. The most dramatic change was in Nevada. Her face had gone pale and she pressed her clenched fists into her stomach.

"Detective Higgins," Sadie said, slowly rising to her feet, "I believe I have the answer to that question." She moved toward Nevada, whose eyes grew large, silently pleading with Sadie. "Nevada, do you want to explain? Or should I?"

Nevada covered her face and burst into tears.

"I don't really care who explains this," Higgins said. "But someone needs to do it now. Ms. Kramer, since *your* prints are also on the phone, why don't you just go ahead and enlighten us all?"

Sadie glanced across the room at Ernie, who was watching the scene intently. She then placed a comforting hand on Nevada's shoulder and looked back at Higgins. "I believe this is Sarah Retsof," she said.

There was a collective gasp of surprise. Alex looked shocked. Penelope and Freda immediately began to whisper. Almost everyone else in the room looked confused, including Roxy, Coop, and Sid. Mitchell looked dismayed, undoubtedly already foreseeing negative publicity. And Ernie looked nothing short of horrified.

"I knew it," Penelope said. "I knew she did it all along." She held her hand out toward Freda, palm up.

Higgins approached Nevada, who became even more hysterical. "I didn't do anything! I would never hurt Brynn, or anyone!"

"You are Sarah Retsof, is that correct?" Higgins said

"Yes, but... but ... not ...." Tears overwhelmed Nevada again.

"Then I'll need you to come with me." Higgins reached for Nevada.

"But I never touched that phone! And I never killed anyone!" She took a step back.

"Then why are your fingerprints on it?" Higgins' question was more of a statement.

"Detective Higgins," Sadie broke in, "I believe she's telling the truth," Sadie said. "She *is* Sarah Retsof, but I'm betting she didn't know the phone she found in her dressing room was Russell's, and she's not the one who killed Brynn Baker."

"Then who did?" Higgins paused, but stayed close to Nevada while he waited for Sadie to answer.

"Someone who badly wanted to protect her identity, for her sake as well as his own," Sadie said.

"And who exactly would that be?" Higgins looked around the room as if someone might confess.

"Her father," Sadie said, directing her attention to Ernie.

"No!" Nevada screamed. "That can't be true." She turned to Ernie. "It's not true, is it, Daddy? You didn't hurt Brynn, did you?"

Ernie crossed the room and knelt down in front of Nevada. "I didn't mean to, baby. But she found out about your past somehow and threatened to tell everyone. Your career would have stalled. I couldn't let that happen to you."

"Or to your own reputation or career," Sadie added. "You wanted to be a good father, to help out your daughter, but you didn't want her past misconduct to taint *your* reputation. So you gave her a new name and a new life."

"Yes, that's right." He looked up at Nevada. "I'm so sorry about the phone. I left it in your dressing room temporarily the night of the dress rehearsal, but it was missing when I went back for it, and I never dreamed you'd touch it."

"What happened, Daddy? Why?"

"I argued with Brynn that day, trying to reason with her, to appeal to her kinder side, but she wouldn't back down. I talked to her again after rehearsal. I thought if she'd relent, I wouldn't need to show up on the catwalk, and she could just think Russell had stood her up."

"Aha," Coop interjected. "That's who I heard yelling from Brynn's dressing room. I just figured it was Sid, as usual."

"Hey!" Sid said, frowning.

"I thought if I met Brynn privately to discuss it later, I could reason with her," Ernie continued.

"So you borrowed Russell's phone," Sadie said, "knowing Russell and Brynn had a habit of meeting after hours on the catwalk. Which I suspect you heard from someone who cleans the theatre at night sometimes and tends to have loose lips, shall we say."

"Uh oh," Penelope said, sinking lower in her seat.

"You sent the text, copying Russell's style because you knew she wouldn't want to talk to you anymore. Then you waited for her on the catwalk," Sadie continued.

"Yes, but I never meant to kill her, I swear," Ernie insisted. "She just wouldn't listen. We argued and struggled, and she went over the edge of the railing."

"Perhaps with a slight push," Higgins commented as he pulled handcuffs from his back pocket, helped Ernie to his feet and secured his wrists. "We'll discuss this further at the station."

Higgins and Ernie left, with Nevada in tow, who insisted on going along. A few cast members called it an evening, the rest were now subdued after all the drama. Sid and Mitchell headed straight to the open bar for stronger drinks. Freda and Penelope began verbally dissecting the entire scenario. And Sadie, Roxy and Coop took a seat together.

"I don't understand how you figured out Ernie was Nevada's father," Roxy said.

"By her last name," Sadie said. "Remember the research I did on the backgrounds of all the execs? Ernie was married once when he was young, just briefly, to a Margaret Retsof."

"OK," Roxy said. "So when Higgins said the name Retsof, you connected it to his former wife's name."

"Exactly," Sadie said. "His Wikipedia page didn't list a child, but we know that site can be unreliable."

"Wow, her stage name, or new identity name, whatever you want to call it..." Coop said. "Nevada Foster. It's a great name. I wonder how he came up with that?"

"Remember he brought her up from Las Vegas?" Sadie said

"Right," Roxy said. "So 'Nevada' for the first name. Clever. But what about 'Foster'?"

"I can explain that, too," Sadie said. Smirking, she retrieved a stack of cocktail napkins and pulled six from the top of the stack. Pulling a pen from her tote bag, she wrote each letter of "Retsof" on a separate napkin and set them in a row across the table. "Go on," she said.

Roxy and Coop looked at the napkins for a moment, and then started moving them around. It only took a couple switches before the jumbled letters took on the new order.

"Clever," Roxy said. "R...E...T...S...O...F" reversed is "F...O...S...T...E...R."

Coco poked her head out of the tote and yowled.

"Yes, Coco," Sadie said. "Clever, indeed."

CHAPTER TWENTY-THREE

Sadie picked up a truffle, popped it in her mouth, closed her eyes, and sighed.

"What do you think?" Amber said. "It might be Matteo's best creation yet: lemon tart with candied pecans?"

"Delicious," Sadie said. "I think there's a bit of ginger in there, too."

"It's good to have you back," Amber said.

"Good to be back, especially after all that cast party commotion. Not to mention yet another discussion with Detective Higgins afterward." Sadie reached for a second truffle, paused in an attempt to resist, and then gave in.

"I still don't understand the whole phone scenario," Amber said. "Why were Nevada's ... er... Sarah's ... fingerprints on the phone and not Ernie's? He's the one who took Russell's phone and sent the message."

"Ernie had already wiped the phone clean. He planned to put it back in Russell's dressing room, but heard someone in the hallway, so left it in Nevada's dressing room sometime during the rehearsal, intending to retrieve it later and return it," Sadie said.

"And then your little canine kleptomaniac put it in your tote bag," Amber said.

"Exactly. Meanwhile, Nevada must have picked it up and set it down again." Sadie eyed the truffles again, this time resisting. "Ernie tried to retrieve it later under the guise of taking Nevada coffee, but it was already in my bag, not that I knew it, of course."

"That's why the police couldn't find it, because *you* had it."

"I'm afraid so," Sadie said.

Amber laughed. "You have to admit it's funny."

"Well, *I* thought so, but Higgins didn't." Sadie said. "You'd think the police could have had a sense of humor about Coco unknowingly swiping murder evidence. It's not like the poor dog was trying to hinder the investigation, after all."

Coco, comfortably curled up on the counter's velvet pillow, let out a sigh and rested her chin on both paws.

Amber looked at Coco. "You do know that's tampering with evidence, don't you, Coco?" She turned back to Sadie. "Dogs can't be charged with that, can they?"

"I wouldn't think so," Sadie said.

"So you were going to turn it over to the detective, but Coco took it out of your tote before you had a chance?" Amber asked.

Sadie nodded. "Yes, because I stopped by the theatre to see the new show flyers before I headed to the police station. Was *that* ever awkward when I went in to give the phone to Higgins! I hadn't told him I was bringing the missing phone, so I just pretended I'd lost a list that I'd planned to bring him."

"You do have a way of getting yourself in *and* out of situations, so I imagine you adlibbed pretty well," Amber said. "Especially with all your recent theatre training," she teased.

"Very funny," Sadie said. "Coco's really the one with the theatre experience now: four performances, all with rave reviews."

"You must be so proud of her," Amber said. "Does this mean she has a future on the stage?"

"Not if I can help it!" Sadie laughed. "But she's a rascal, for sure. Who knows what she'll get into next?"

"Well, whatever it is, it's bound to be interesting," Amber said.

Sadie patted Coco's head and scratched her behind the ears. "Yes, I imagine it will be."

Individual Chocolate Lava Cakes

Makes 6

INGREDIENTS

Center
2 ounces bittersweet chocolate (around 60% cacao), chopped
1/4 cup heavy cream

Cake
4 ounces bittersweet chocolate (around 60% cacao), chopped
1/2 cup (4 ounces) unsalted butter
2 eggs plus 2 egg yolks
1/3 cup granulated sugar
1/2 teaspoon vanilla extract
1/4 cup cake flour

Garnish
Whipped cream
Raspberries

DIRECTIONS

Center (must be done ahead of time)
Heat the heavy cream in a small sauce pan just until bubbles start to form around the edges, then remove from heat. Do not boil.

Place 2 ounces of bittersweet chopped chocolate in a heat-proof bowl and pour the hot cream over. Allow to sit for 5 minutes, then stir until smooth. (No need to wash the sauce pan, you'll need it for the cake.)

Refrigerate the chocolate mixture for 2 hours or until firm, then divide into 6 balls. Return to refrigerator until needed.

Cake

Preheat the oven to 400 degrees (F).

Spray 6 4-ounce ramekins with non-stick cooking spray.

Melt the butter in a small sauce pan then remove from heat.

Add the 4 ounces of chopped bittersweet chocolate to the pan and whisk until melted and smooth. Set aside.

In the bowl of a standing mixer, add the eggs, egg yolks, sugar, and vanilla. Beat on medium high speed for about 5 minutes, until the mixture is thick and light colored.

Gently fold in the melted chocolate and butter mixture.

Add the flour and stir just until combined.

Spoon the batter into the prepared ramekins and place a chilled chocolate ball into the center of each one.

Place ramekins on a baking sheet and bake for about 15 minutes or until cake is firm to the touch.

Remove from oven and allow to cool for 5 minutes.

Run a knife around the inside of ramekin, place a small dessert plate over top, then flip over and remove the ramekin. Repeat with each one.

Garnish with fresh whipped cream and raspberries.

ACKNOWLEDGEMENTS

I owe tremendous thanks to many people for helping bring *A Flair for Drama* to life.

Elizabeth Christy's exceptional editing skills have helped make Sadie and Coco's theatre adventure shine. Keri Knutson of Alchemy Book Covers and Design created the lively, colorful cover concept for the Sadie Kramer Flair Mysteries; her artistic talent is always appreciated. Credit goes to both Richard Houston and Tim Renfrow for formatting. Beta readers Jay Garner, Karen Putnam and Carol Anderson provided insight into plot development. Carol gets extra credit for her keen proofreading eye.

If you love Chocolate Lava Cake as much as Sadie does, you'll enjoy the recipe included after the final chapter. Thanks go to Kim Davis and her *Cinnamon & Sugar and a Little Bit of Murder* blog for this delicious addition.

As always, I am grateful for the constant support of family, friends and readers. Their encouragement guarantees Sadie and Coco will have more adventures in the future.

CPSIA information can be obtained
at www.ICGtesting.com
Printed in the USA
FSOW02n1607230517
34442FS